Romance ...
is that what makes us
fall in love?

Or, is it falling in love
that makes everything
romantic?

Come ... rediscover romance
and fall in love ...
with Ponder Romance.

Also from Ponder Romance

Autumn's Eve   by Jordanna Boston
This roller-coaster romance will keep you chuckling as one man's misery becomes a whole town's fortune when he rolls his truck outside a remote Canadian community.

Sand Pirates   by Ellis Hoff
A page-turning potion of hide-and-seek on an island too small for criminals but just the right size for romance.

Oh Susannah

Selena Mindus

A Ponder Romance

Published by Ponder Publishing Inc.

Oh Susannah

A Ponder Romance Book
Published by Ponder Publishing Inc.
P.O. Box 23037 RPO McGillivray
Winnipeg, Manitoba
R3T 5S3 Canada

U.S. Address: 60 East 42nd Street, Suite 1166, New York, New York, 101655
Internet address: http://www.ponderpublishing.com

Cover Photography: Copyright D. Barton. Used by permission.

Cover by: PeR Design

ISBN 0-9681587-0-6

Printed in Canada

One

"Semchuck, Bert and Ada." Susannah frowned at the names on the wooden sign and drew her flashlight back inside the car. If she wasn't so tired and frustrated, she'd probably find the situation amusing.

When she had viewed the cottage with the real estate agent, she had thought it would be easy to find on her own. She had even noted the names of her immediate neighbours. She shook her head as she read the scrap of paper once more: site 304 Lee River Road – next to the Semchuks. What she had failed to notice originally was that two other Semchuks also lived along the road. And to make things more confusing, overgrown brush obscured most of the property markers, and those that were visible seemed to follow no logical sequence.

"Are we there yet, mom?" a sleepy voice asked from the back seat.

"I don't know, Calvin. I hope so."

"I wanna go home," another voice whimpered while Susannah opened her door and stepped out into the night.

"Chad, honey, this is home; our new home," Susannah assured, then muttered to herself, "I just have to find it." She poked her head back inside.

"I'm just going over there by those bushes to look for our marker."

Perfect! Susannah thought, swatting at bugs as she approached the brush, gravel crunching beneath her shoes. Windless, humid and billions of mosquitoes! Glaring into the darkness, she wielded her flashlight about impatiently, wishing she could somehow command it to illuminate her cottage and the river she knew had to be there ... somewhere ... was that a glimmer? She passed her light over the area again and stepped into the shrubbery for a closer look. She sighed with relief at the small sign. "I'm home!"

"Mommy! Mommy! A bear!" her sons screamed from inside the car.

Susannah quickly spun around and surveyed the surrounding area but saw no sign of a bear. Nevertheless, she hurried back to the car. "What bear?" she asked breathlessly through the car window. As her sons gave opposing declarations of the bear's whereabouts, she began to suspect that although they were in prime black-bear country, it was probably nothing more than shadows in the moonlight and overactive imaginations.

"Well, if it was a bear," she interrupted what was rapidly developing into a full-blown argument, "it's gone now, guys."

Calvin quickly turned to scan the darkness beyond the windows. "What if it's not gone, Mom?"

"Yeah," her youngest persisted, on the verge of tears.

"Chad," she soothed, "it won't hurt us if we leave it alone, and besides, bears don't like loud noise and you two made lots of that." She reached in through the car window and brushed the hair from his forehead, knowing how tired he was. "It's probably long gone by now. And guess what?"

"What?" he sniffed.

"I've found the cottage!"

"Finally!" Calvin snorted in disgust.

"How about if you guys wait here while I go down and open it up?"

"Nooo! Don't leave us!" both boys howled.

Susannah's sigh was heavy and bordering on impatience. Her vision of the move to their new home had not included having to struggle blindly down an unfamiliar path in the pitch of night with two frightened boys clinging to her legs while a bear possibly prowled nearby.

Everything would have gone smoothly if they had arrived before dark like she had intended, but amidst a multitude of last-minute preparations, she had forgotten to buy groceries, a mistake she had fortunately discovered before they left. The shopping had postponed their arrival long enough to make it dark by the time they reached Lee River, which had only added to her difficulty in locating the cottage.

Susannah handed Calvin the flashlight, hoping the task of lighting their way would keep his mind off any real or imagined bears. And with typical exuberance, he proceeded to illuminate treetops, bushes and anything of interest but the path. Keeping her temper in check required extra patience as she struggled down the hill with Chad clutching anxiously at her arm and Calvin bounding around in front of her.

Finally, the path opened to a clearing and a small cedar cottage silhouetted in the moonlight. If she hadn't been so eager to drop into the nearest bed, Susannah might have taken time to appreciate the view, but instead she unlocked the aged but solid wooden door and stepped inside.

Flicking on the light, she surveyed her new home

while the boys pushed past her and ran from room to room, investigating closets and cupboards. The most prominent room was the small but cheery living room furnished with an old colonial sofa and mismatching, overstuffed armchairs that sagged from years of use. A worn braided rug, on which rested a small coffee table, warmed the room. A potbelly stove waited patiently for winter against a brick wall which separated two small bedrooms. The master bedroom at the opposite end of the living room boasted an old iron bed, a small vanity and another braided rug, while the smaller rooms had matching twin beds and a chest of drawers. A tiny kitchenette with old appliances and an equally old chrome-framed table and chairs set completed the cottage.

Definitely an interior decorator's nightmare, Susannah thought as she took in the plaid drapes and the cheap, black-velvet paintings hanging on the walls, but it was a welcome change from the sterile luxury that had been their ultramodern condominium. Here the boys could track in mud and leave their toys lying about without ruining the carpet. Here Susannah could be at ease; redecorating could wait.

"Calvin," she called as she headed back outside, "please open the door for me when I return." She had scarcely made it to the car when the boys began to bawl from behind the cottage screen door. Hauling two heavy suitcases, she hobbled back and reassured them she was not going to be eaten by a bear. Their hysterics escalated with each trip, necessitating her decision to bring in only the essentials and leave the remainder for morning. Too exhausted to sort her groceries, Susannah shoved them, bags and all, into the refrigerator.

Her sons were chasing each other around the

living room and quarrelling over which bedroom would belong to whom. Using the timeworn "one potato, two potato ..." she resolved the dispute and amidst giggles and horseplay managed to manoeuvre them into their pyjamas and, at last, their beds.

She headed towards her own bedroom and left the light off, not wanting to irritate her already throbbing head. Fumbling through her suitcase in the dark, she tossed aside several items in search of a nightie. Finding none and too exhausted to care, she stripped naked and crawled into bed.

A warm breeze caressed Susannah's cheek, nudging her from her slumber. She opened her eyes and gazed out the window, slowly taking in the dark, tree-lined slope that led to the river's edge where cedar lawn chairs bathed in the sunlight. The river, which shone in the clear morning sky, was a bright blue. She yawned, breathing in the fragrant country air drifting in through the open window. She smiled and snuggled back into the pillows and spread an arm across the cool bed, realizing that for the first time since Steven's death, it was not so painfully vacant. Her smile deepened. Her instincts had been right. Leaving everything behind and moving to Lee River was going to be the start of a fresh new life.

Susannah sprang out of bed and grinned at the assortment of clothes strewn about. The nightie which had eluded her last night lay atop a pile of clothes. She was about to don a pair of walking shorts when she spied a pair of denim cutoffs. She giggled as she picked them up along with a skimpy tube top. It was so isolated here she could probably run around buck naked; besides she felt wonderfully free, almost reckless.

The cutoffs, resurrected from younger years, were

significantly shorter than she remembered. She had lost so much weight in the year and a half since her husband's death that she could fit into them now. She twisted around in front of the mirror and grinned at the slim but shapely figure. Not bad for a woman nearing thirty, she thought as she patted herself on the butt.

She pulled closer to the mirror to examine her face and decided not to bother with makeup, thankful that her big, smoky-grey eyes and full lips were adornments in themselves. And who was there to run into around here anyway?

The sound of clanking cutlery told her the boys were up and looking for breakfast. Quickly tying her shimmering and shoulder-length auburn hair into a ponytail, she joined them in the kitchen.

"Hey guys! What's up?" she said as she squeezed Chad's shoulders and ruffled Calvin's hair.

"Mom, can we just have cereal?" Calvin asked as he poured milk into a bowl of Rice Krispies and placed it in front of his younger brother who was already seated and waiting to be served.

"Yeah," said Chad, "we wanna go exploring!"

Susannah contemplated her sons. Nine-year-old Calvin had coped with his father's death by becoming a surrogate father to Chad, who, although only one year younger, had correspondingly regressed. I guess I haven't been much of a mother lately, she lamented as she opened the fridge door and then closed her eyes in disgust. A toppled bag of groceries had freed melted chocolate ice cream to drip everywhere.

"I didn't know how to clean it up," Calvin offered guiltily, as if he were somehow responsible.

Susannah closed the fridge door, grabbed the Rice Krispies and sat down beside him. She pinched his cheek. "Well, we're just not going to worry about it right now."

She had other things to worry about, she mused as she munched. The sticky brown goo inside her fridge was a grim reminder that she was going to have to learn how to manage a household. Out here in the middle of nowhere, without any help – the task seemed overwhelming. She couldn't cook – Steven had always done that; she couldn't clean – a housekeeper had always seen to that. And anything else around the house that needed tending to had been taken care of by Steven so that she would be free to devote herself to the university courses she took at night. She sighed dejectedly. A degree in Business Administration wasn't going to be of much use out here.

You'll get better at this, she chided herself, vaguely aware that Calvin was taking away her finished cereal bowl and placing it in the sink with his and Chad's.

"Can we go exploring now?" Calvin asked, returning to the table as Chad echoed the question.

Susannah contemplated their animated faces before her smoky eyes wandered around the cottage, bypassing the fridge with its ghastly contents and stopping at the dirty dishes on the counter. Their suitcases had yet to be unpacked, a film of dust covered every piece of furniture, and the car was still full of boxes. The light-heartedness that had greeted her upon waking was waning and a heavy depression threatened to overtake her. No, she commanded herself, as if exorcising the looming blackness, this was the first bright morning the three of them had seen in countless months and she was darned if they would waste it with trifles like settling in.

"Let's go exploring!" she announced with a wide

grin.

The morning sun was already heavy with heat when Susannah unstrapped the bicycles from the car roof. Pushing aside baggage and other paraphernalia in the trunk, she tossed each of the boys a helmet and eyed the road warily. She had scarcely strapped her own helmet into place when she realized that Calvin and Chad were already riding away. Biting back her usual lecture on road safety, she mounted her own bike and followed closely behind, ever watchful for oncoming traffic.

It was soon evident to Susannah, however, that the only things approaching from any direction were the sounds of the forest and that which lived in it. Susannah waved in return to a woman tending her flower garden and concluded that she must be Ada Semchuk, her neighbour.

The Semchuks' cottage was as isolated as her own, as were all the cottages along this particular stretch, one of only a few remaining pockets of wilderness on the river. And that's why she had chosen it. Lee River, because of its unusual calm and lake-like character, was generally cramped with cottagers who preferred the quiet river over nearby Lake Winnipeg, Manitoba's largest and the world's eleventh largest freshwater lake, which could be as fierce and unpredictable as an ocean.

Susannah chuckled at some of the more inventive property markers along the road. While some cottagers simply branded their family name onto a varnished piece of wood that was either nailed to a post or hung from a tree, it was unspoken cottage-country tradition to baptize your haven with an elaborate name and illustrate it accordingly. One such place, "Castle Grove," boasted a miniature castle which had been chiselled out of a boulder. Another, entitled "Happy Haven," was flagged by hundreds of "smile" faces painted on any and every surface.

"Hey, Mom, you should see this one," both boys called from further up the road. They had stopped in front of what resembled a pagoda.

Susannah was waving to them when the blast of a horn and a squeal of brakes startled her from behind. Simultaneously, her front tire hit a rut in the road, and before she could replace her hand on the handle bar, the bike was careening downhill with Susannah struggling to regain control. Unable to halt her bumpy descent, she abandoned the bike, but the momentum kept her rolling downhill behind it. Her tumble was finally impeded by an oak tree.

She could hear her sons screaming with terror while she lay wondering if she were dead. Three pairs of legs appeared on the crest of the hill; two sets she recognized as her sons while the other, darkly tanned and deeply muscled, began making their way down to her.

"Don't move!" an equally masculine voice commanded.

Susannah raised her eyes. He was shirtless and wearing denim cutoffs, and his deeply tanned torso was a mass of muscles liberally covered with black hair.

"Are you alright?" he asked as he knelt down beside her. All she could do was stare. His face was even more tanned than his chest, and his eyes were the darkest brown she had ever seen. There was a hint of Native Indian in the strong, angular cheekbones, and Susannah wondered if he were Metis. A girl could get lost in those eyes, she thought. She drew in a sharp breath. Had she spoken aloud, or was she dazed from her tumble?

His hair was the same deep shade of brown as his eyes and wavy. She was staring at it hard. She did not want to look into his eyes again. She tried to sit up, but a stab of pain prevented her attempt.

"Let me help you." He took her hand, and placing his arm under her shoulder, began to lift her up.

Susannah steadied herself by resting a hand on his chest which, she discovered, was damp with perspiration and warm, as if he'd been working hard. Mesmerized, she flattened her hand against his skin and found that the muscles were hard and thick.

"Are you sure you're alright?" he asked again, amusement in his eyes.

As if scorched, Susannah pushed away from him.

"I'm fine," she spat, brushing the leaves and dirt from her cutoffs. Her legs and arms were scraped and bruised. She dared to look up at him again, but his dark eyes were slowly wandering up her legs to her face.

She became acutely aware that her tube top had all but completely slid down, leaving little to his imagination. Grabbing hold of it, she pulled it up, shaking everything into place. Susannah was not buxom, but nature had been generous just the same.

He was grinning now.

Mortified, Susannah screeched, "What the heck did you think you were doing driving like a maniac?"

He continued grinning. "I was well within the speed limit. Perhaps you weren't paying attention."

Susannah wanted to smack the smile off his face. "Perhaps you're just a bad driver," she snapped.

She bent down to retrieve her helmet, which had somehow come off during her tumble. She knew that he continued to study her with interest, and her clothing suddenly seemed skimpy. She sorely regretted not having opted for the T-shirt and walking shorts, but giggled inanely when she remembered having contemplated going buck naked.

"Maybe I should give you a ride home," he suggested. "Your bikes would fit in the back of my pickup."

"I'll be alright as long as you keep off the road!"

Her side ached from the bump against the tree, and the bruises were beginning to throb. Feeling faint, she closed her eyes and leaned against the tree, waiting for the dizziness to pass.

"I can't let you go in the condition you're in. You're liable to cause another accident." His grin was only half amused.

Incensed, but unable to think of a biting retort, Susannah stuck up her nose, pushed past him and commenced to clamber up the hill.

"Have you forgotten your bike, or would you like me to carry it up for you?" he asked, his mirth barely concealed.

"Please," Susannah ground out, not bothering to turn around and angrier still at having forgotten her bike.

He followed behind, chuckling under his breath, and she wished her cutoffs were not so short.

"Are you okay, Mom?" Calvin asked when she reached the crest of the hill. Chad stood beside him in silent terror.

Anger momentarily forgotten, she hugged them to her. "Don't you guys worry about your mom. I'm fine, but let's go home."

He parked the bicycle beside her. "Are you sure I can't give you a lift?" he asked, sounding concerned despite the grin that continued to play at the corners of his mouth.

She kept her back to him as she mounted her bike, partly because she wanted to be rude, but mostly because she didn't want him to see her grimace in pain. "You've done enough for one day, I think," was her snooty reply as she pedalled away, the boys jumping quickly on their bikes to follow.

Two

Susannah was stiff and sore the next morning. And even the simple task of preparing breakfast provided ample opportunity for muscles to scream. However, if she didn't want to spend another night tossing and turning in the cold, she'd have to light a fire, and ultimately, that meant chopping wood.

The only source of heat in the cottage was a wood-burning stove in the living room, and although the summer days could be sweltering, the damp night air tended to turn chilly. The cabin was winterized and the stove more than able to warm it during Manitoba's harsh winters, but if she didn't want to worry about always having wood on hand, she would eventually have to install electric heaters.

She eyed a pile of logs by the edge of the clearing. Perhaps for now, extra blankets on their beds would suffice. The boys hadn't complained about the cold, not that she'd had a chance to ask them. They had run off after breakfast to explore and were most likely deeply entrenched in some neighbour's yard by now.

Besides, she really didn't know how to chop wood, although she supposed it was rather simple. Suddenly it was a challenge. After all, Steven had said if the axe was sharp, anyone could do it.

She remembered seeing an axe in the shed and wondered if it was sharp. How to tell, she wasn't sure, short of running a finger along the blade. Instead she chose to try it on a log. Susannah stood back, legs apart, and made a mighty swing, missing the log completely and imbedding the axe in the ground.

"I can do this," she told herself. Her second swing netted a wood chip. Hardly enough to cause a sliver, she lamented.

She imagined this would be a breeze for the man who'd nearly run her down yesterday. He'd be shirtless, his tanned muscles glistening with sweat while he laboured. Startled by her thoughts, she swung the axe again, this time barely missing her own leg.

She grit her teeth. "I can do this." With another determined swing the axe hit its target, lodged itself in the log and refused to budge.

Serious doubts as to Steven's expertise crept into her mind. Steven was a banker. Their vacations had consisted of Caribbean cruises and trips to Disneyland. The closest he ever came to the "great outdoors" was the occasional fire he lit in their condominium fireplace, and that with firewood already split, bundled and delivered to their door.

She chuckled, recalling more clearly now that they had been watching a log-chopping contest at a winter festival when Steven, in response to her remarks on the contestants' strength, had asserted that if the axe was sharp anyone could chop wood.

"This axe looks pretty sharp to me," she grumbled, bracing a foot against the log and yanking on the axe, aware that a boat was pulling up to her dock. She stopped and quickly wiped the sweat from her brow, wishing she had at least one split log to show for her labour. A rather loud laugh had her turning towards the dock and staring with disbelief.

"Well, well! If the widow who bought my cottage isn't also the little terror on two wheels!" Susannah couldn't help but feel a sense of deja vu as she watched those same legs, only now in jeans, climb up the river bank towards her.

"How are you feeling today?" he asked, stopping close and smiling down at her, his dark eyes veiled by sunglasses.

"Stiff ... my bruises hurt," she stammered, rubbing an elbow and stepping back. She wanted to pluck off his sunglasses, which she suspected shielded amusement.

"I'm glad it's nothing more serious," he said gravely as he reached out to examine her elbow.

"Well, it's no thanks to you!" she snorted, pulling her arm back.

He laughed. "Maybe we should start over. How about if I promise to drive more carefully, and we'll pretend we've just met for the first time?"

Was he patronizing her? She supposed yesterday's mishap wasn't entirely his fault. She was also feeling guilty for her rudeness yesterday.

"I suppose we could try," she offered slowly.

He removed his sunglasses. "I'm Gabriel Desjarlais."

His eyes were even darker than she remembered, and she felt equally lost in them today. "Susannah James," she answered breathlessly, hardly aware that she was extending her hand.

He took it and held it. "You should use gloves."

"Gloves?"

He nodded in the direction of the axe. "It would protect your hands from blisters, which I see you already have." He ran a finger over one.

His touch sent shivers through Susannah, and she snatched her hand back. "What did you mean ... I bought your cottage?"

"I nearly bought this place for my mother. She's retired and we thought it would be perfect for her. She's lived on Lee River most of her life."

"Surely my cottage wasn't the only one available," Susannah snorted.

Gabriel shook his dark head. "No, but my farm's directly across the river, and it would have been easy to keep an eye on her."

"That doesn't mean it was your cottage."

"Actually it was. I had a verbal agreement with the owners. My lawyer was drawing up the documents when they phoned to say it had been sold to someone who paid more than their asking price." He raised an eyebrow.

She raised her chin. "I was told they had several other offers. So I offered more. Besides, I liked the place. It's perfect for us."

Why was she justifying her actions to him? Was it her fault the previous owners had been unscrupulous? "Perhaps you shouldn't have been so trusting?"

"Perhaps you're right. However, we do things differently in the country. A person's word is taken seriously."

"Why didn't you fight for your rights?"

"My mother was no longer upset when she heard a young widow had bought it." He paused, the corners of his mouth betraying a grin. "And now I don't mind so much either."

Susannah frowned. "Are you saying your original intention in coming here today was to argue with me over the property?" She was beginning to regret having dropped her animosity towards him.

Gabriel flashed a smile. "Not at all. I was just curious. Besides I figured you and the lady I ran into yesterday might be one and the same. I wanted to make sure you were okay."

Susannah massaged a tender elbow and replied stiffly, "I appreciate your concern, but I'm really quite fine now, thank you."

"Mom!" Chad interrupted. "Look what the lady next door gave us! And the man said he'd fix your bike!" Both boys came running to her with warm, chocolate chip cookies.

"She made them herself," Calvin said with awe as he reverently offered one to his mother.

"What are you boys doing accepting cookies from a stranger?" Susannah demanded.

Gabriel chuckled. "Bert and Ada Semchuk have been our friends for as long as I can remember. Their farm was next door to mine."

"Well, they are still strangers to us," Susannah put in tartly. "And for that matter, so are you. They were wrong to accept the cookies."

"Perhaps," he replied, "but as I said before, things are different in the country. Why don't you meet Ada for yourself, and then the boys can keep their cookies?"

She studied the rugged lines of Gabriel's face and found no insincerity. "I suppose you're right," she relented.

He gave her a gentle smile. "I don't think you'll regret it. I'd introduce you myself, but I have to be getting back. The hired help will be arriving shortly."

Susannah was relieved. His presence unnerved her. He was too handsome, or too big, or too something.

"What kind of farm do you have?" she asked to break the silence as she walked him back to the dock.

"Berry. Our main crop is strawberries, but we also

grow raspberries and blueberries."

Susannah laughed as Gabriel climbed into his boat. "I'm afraid I'd eat myself silly if I owned that kind of farm. I absolutely love berries."

His dark eyes locked with her soft grey ones. "Well then, I'll have to make sure you have your fill."

And then he was gone, his boat churning up the water behind him.

Susannah decided to follow Gabriel's advice and introduce herself to the neighbours. Calvin and Chad escorted her, alternately running ahead to announce her imminent arrival and returning to take her hands and pull her along as if haste was of critical importance.

The Semchuks were standing in the shade at the edge of their clearing. They greeted Susannah as if they had long awaited the opportunity to meet her.

"Well, here she is at last. We've heard a great deal about you from your darling little sons," said Ada Semchuk, a robustly plump woman whose bulk and thick grey hair were in stark contrast with her husband's gaunt and balding frame. "I was thrilled to discover you don't bake because my own grandsons live in Vancouver – why my sons had to move out there I'll never know but I guess British Columbia's the land of milk and honey – and I never get to bake for anyone. I gave up trying to fatten up old Bert here long ago. And as you can see," she paused for a heavy breath and slapped her hips, "I certainly don't need it. Anyway I just popped these cookies in the oven right away."

The woman grabbed Susannah's elbow and pushed her towards the house. "Your lads – what lovely fellows, all that blond hair and blue eyes –

said you had an accident with your bicycle yesterday."

Susannah wondered if the woman was going to
stop for air and how the boys had managed to tell her
anything. She found herself in Mrs. Semchuk's
kitchen and pushed into a chair. A steaming cup of
tea and a plate of warm cookies were placed in front
of her.

"From the description of the truck, I would
imagine that was Gabriel Desjarlais," she continued.
"Now, there's a handsome man. And not married ...
too busy helping his mother raise them four sisters of
his, I guess. But the youngest's just gone off to
university, so I imagine he'll have more time to look
for a wife now that it's just him and his mom at
home."

Not knowing how to respond, Susannah sipped at
her tea and nibbled on a cookie. "Did you put
anything on those scrapes?" Ada inquired as she
brought out a bottle of antiseptic. "Bert, why don't
you go and have a look at the girl's bike? Calvin told
me something's broke on it. Seems the handle bar
got all twisted or some darn thing."

Bert nodded his head in assent and shuffled out the
door. Susannah ate another cookie. "It must be awful
lonesome for you. Your sons said their dad got killed
in a car accident, some car ran a red light," Ada
rambled on as she dabbed Susannah's scrapes with
the antiseptic. "Damned drunk drivers. That's one
thing you can say about Gabriel Desjarlais, he was
always a clear-thinking, responsible boy. Never once
got into a bit of trouble. My own boys could have
followed his example. Oh, they turned out alright,
but I think they're why my hair is grey now. You just
wait, those boys of yours are gonna need a man to
keep them in line."

Susannah was getting the distinct impression the woman's line of conversation was headed in a specific direction.

"They said Gabriel was over to talk to you just now. Wouldn't that be funny if he ended up marrying you?"

Susannah tried to control the blush she felt creeping over her face.

"And here you are living in the very house he wanted to buy for his mother – she was my neighbour, you know." Ada abruptly finished her soliloquy and was now looking to Susannah for comment.

As much as Susannah wanted to refute Ada's misguided notion of a romance between herself and Gabriel Desjarlais, she decided the best way to deal with her was to simply nod her head in agreement and eat the cookies. Besides, she did not want to give the woman more to gossip with than the little she already had.

Bert rescued her by coming in to announce that Susannah's bike was now in working order and to ask if there was anything else she wanted repaired. With a "no thank you," Susannah stood up to leave, realizing to her own horror and Ada's delight that she had consumed the entire plate of cookies.

"I'll get another batch in the oven right away so you can have some with your dinner," Ada said as she patted Susannah's arm.

"Now, Ada," Bert admonished, "don't you get carried away with your baking. It won't be so easy to marry her off to Gabriel if she's fat." He winked at Susannah.

Wishing to discourage further discussion of Gabriel Desjarlais, Susannah insisted it really was time for her to leave and made a hasty retreat out the door.

As she followed the path towards home, she shook her head in disbelief over Ada's eager matchmaking. Susannah hardly knew Gabriel Desjarlais, and the little she did know, she wasn't altogether sure she liked. And as for him, his only interest in her was the cottage which he thought she had usurped from him.

Had she? Was she a callous monster who tore homes out from under the feet of senior citizens? How could anyone expect her to have known about Gabriel's mother? Did anyone care that she needed a quiet place to recover from the loss of her husband?

Tears filled Susannah's eyes. When Steven died, everyone had advised her to maintain life exactly as it had always been. They said it would help both her and the boys come to terms with his absence.

And so she had continued as Branch Manager at the bank where she had first met Steven. She had been fresh out of high school, a mere eighteen when they had married. They worked together for years, until eventually Steven was transferred to another branch and Susannah took over his position, sitting behind what had been his desk in his office. After his death, going to work each day became a torturous ordeal of following his ghost through her every motion.

Staying at home turned out to be no better. His chair across the dinner table was glaringly empty. The clothes smelled of him and every evening his absence cried out from the vacant place beside her pillow. Her life became one endless day after another, a lifetime of nothingness yawning before her.

It was her sons who pulled her back to the land of the living. They had lost their father, but in another sense, their mother also. This realization came via a phone call from the school guidance counsellor who informed Susannah that Calvin and Chad were bullying younger children. Did she have any idea why? the counsellor had asked. She had hung up the phone, knowing why and also knowing what she had to do. And so here she was at Lee River ... starting over.

Already it was proving to be the right decision. She felt free and alive. Everything was new and fresh, from their rustic, outdoor surroundings, to the inner quiet of the cottage which was already fully furnished when she bought it. Into it they brought only their most cherished possessions and anything of necessity that the cottage didn't provide. Everything else was either sold or given away.

Both her own parents and her in-laws thought she was crazy. What about the boys? they had grilled her. Is it safe out there? Didn't she want to be near her family for support? I'm only an hour and a half away, she had argued. The country is by far safer and friendlier than the city, and it was time she learned to stand on her own two feet. As for the boys ... already her arguments were proving correct because for the first time in months they were excited and happy. Full of life. And she had time to bond with them ... be there for them. Tears prickled behind her eyes. No, she would not feel guilty. This was meant to be her home. As for Gabriel, he'd just have to accept it. She certainly wasn't going to lose sleep over it.

Three

High above, an axe glistened menacingly as it readied to strike. Unable to flee, Susannah rolled away, narrowly escaping it's blow. Someone was singing "Oh Susannah! Don't you cry for me ..." Again the axe shimmered above her. She opened her mouth to scream for Steven, but no sound emerged. Where was Steven? Why did he not come?

Susannah bolted upright in bed, her brow damp with perspiration. It was only a dream ... or was it? She could hear the whistled archaic refrains from "Oh Susannah" and the rhythmic thud of an axe. Looking out her window, she saw Gabriel Desjarlais chopping wood while Calvin and Chad chattered gaily and stacked the split logs.

Seizing her terry bathrobe, she stormed out of bed and stomped down the hill, slamming the screen door behind her. Bringing herself to an abrupt halt in front of Gabriel, she spat, "If I had wanted your help, I would have asked!"

Gabriel stopped whistling but did not look up as he thrust the axe into another log. "I know that," came his simple response through laboured breaths.

"You're out of luck if you think I'm some lonely widow who will sleep with you because she's grateful for a small favour!"

Gabriel tossed a piece of wood onto the growing pile beside him and then leaning on the axe, turned to Susannah. His eyes slowly scanned the length of her body, and he threw back his head and laughed.

Susannah bristled. Granted, having just rolled out of bed, she was not at her best, but she wasn't that unattractive, was she?

Wiping the sweat from his forehead with an arm, Gabriel chuckled some more and shook his head at her in disbelief. "First of all, honey, chopping this wood is no small favour. I've been at it for two hours already!"

Susannah proceeded to interject, but Gabriel cut her off. "And second, I'm only being neighbourly. I certainly did not expect Bert Semchuk to sleep with me after chopping wood for him last winter."

Susannah felt a twinge of guilt. It was possible she had jumped to conclusions. She was on the verge of apologizing when she saw that the laughter had not yet left his eyes. Her mouth fell open with indignation, then closed with a saccharine smile. "Well, now that we have the matter of your sexual orientation cleared up, would you like some coffee?"

Gabriel grinned. "I take it black." His grin deepened. "And I highly doubt that there was ever a question in your mind."

Susannah turned and huffed back up the hill to make the coffee she had so foolishly offered. Why had she not just sent him packing?

Okay, so maybe he wasn't like some of Steven's friends, who, after his death, one by one came calling under the pretext of doing her some small favour. However, Susannah's idea of gratitude and theirs differed greatly, leaving her suspect of any man's intentions towards her. So why should she have believed Gabriel was any different?

She sighed as she entered the kitchen and commenced preparing the coffee, absently popping fresh raspberries into her mouth while she worked. She popped another berry into her mouth and stopped mid-chew, letting her eyes wander towards the basket of berries filled to overflowing and sitting on her kitchen counter.

She blushed, remembering Gabriel's promise to provide her with her fill. Susannah swallowed hard and pushed the basket away, then chastised herself. The man was a berry farmer. He likely brought berries to all of his neighbours.

Waiting for the coffee, she searched her room for something to wear and vacillated between shorts and a sundress, finally opting for the sundress since it was definitely more feminine. Its emerald green would accent her auburn hair and darken her grey eyes while its simple lines remained uncontrived.

Twice Susannah removed the dress and put on the shorts, telling herself it was ridiculous to fuss about her appearance for a man who was merely being neighbourly. In the end, femininity won out, and she wore the dress, twisting her hair into a French braid and securing it with a green bow. A light brush of mascara to her already long lashes and a touch of blush to her cheeks was all she allowed herself, intuitively knowing a man like Gabriel would find heavy makeup unattractive.

She poured two cups of coffee and carried them outside. Gabriel was still splitting logs and whistling "Oh Susannah." He stopped working when he saw her, but appeared not to notice the pains she had taken with her appearance.

"Do you know the words?" Susannah asked, disappointed by his indifference.

"No, not really."

"Me neither." She seated herself at the picnic table. Gabriel sat down beside her, his knee almost imperceptibly touching her leg, and took a sip from his mug of coffee.

Susannah searched wildly for a topic of conversation, but could not focus on anything other than the feathery touch of his skin against hers. If she slid her leg away, would he notice? What would he think if she didn't move her leg?

Gabriel took another gulp of coffee and relaxed against the table, causing his knee to lean against her leg even more. Susannah fought the panic overtaking her. The heat from his skin was rising up her leg to her face. Terrified she would be unable to control the impulse to jump up from the table, Susannah cleared her throat and pretended to shift to a more comfortable position.

"So," she began with artificial lightness, "I take it you're not needed on the farm this morning?"

Gabriel remained silent for a moment, but couldn't hide the amusement tugging at his eyes. "Well," he replied slowly, pausing to finish the last of his coffee before his eyes locked with hers, "when an attractive woman tells me she could get lost in my eyes, I figure she should be given an opportunity to do so."

Susannah choked on her coffee, nearly spilling it over them both. "I must have been delirious from shock," she sputtered, feeling the heat of her crimson face.

"I was rather hoping you weren't," he drawled lazily and then laughed. "I can't remember when I've seen a woman blush as much as you!"

Susannah leaped to her feet. "And you're so experienced, living out in the country, taking care of your mother and sisters?" she snarled.

Gabriel lounged against the table and grinned up

at her. "You're attempting to change the topic. Why don't you just admit you're attracted to me?"

Susannah huffed. "Aren't you conceited? And besides, I thought you said you weren't interested in me."

He rose from the picnic table and brought himself so close to her Susannah could feel the heat of his body. She fought the urge to step back, aware that it would only produce that knowing amusement in his eyes.

"We were discussing your attraction for me, not mine for you, but just to clarify things for you, Susannah, all I recall saying was that I didn't expect to sleep with you as payment for chopping wood." He grinned slowly. "Both services are free."

Susannah's blush spread to the very roots of her hair. She stood blinking at Gabriel in wide-eyed surprise, her mouth agape. "I think you overrate yourself, Mr. Desjarlais," she said through clenched teeth before turning on her heels.

"Susannah!" Gabriel called up to her as she headed towards the cabin, his voice rich with humour. "I may have been busy with my responsibilities, but I've been no hermit. I have enough experience to know you're so attracted to me that it's written all over you – right down to that cute little dress you're wearing!"

She slammed the screen door behind her, his laughter ringing in her ears. Tears of frustration brimmed her eyes and she choked down a sob. Entering her room to change, her anger surprisingly shifted towards Steven.

This was all his fault. If he hadn't gone and died on her, she wouldn't even be at Lee River, and Gabriel Desjarlais would have to find someone else to pick on. Brushing an errant tear aside, Susannah angrily donned her shorts, blaming Steven that she hadn't worn them in the first place. Steven had been the only man in her life, and she was not equipped to deal with her present situation.

Plunking herself on the bed, she shifted her gaze towards the window where Gabriel was in plain view. She toyed with the idea of hiding herself inside the cabin for the rest of the day, but the sight of him labouring at the woodpile made her stomach flutter.

"Oh no!" she sobbed as she buried her face into her hands. Maybe Gabriel was right. Maybe she was attracted to him. But how could she be? Wasn't her love for Steven as strong as ever? And as for Gabriel, he hadn't actually said he was interested in her. All he had said was that he would willingly accommodate her if she so desired.

She dabbed at her eyes with a Kleenex. She supposed she should be offended by his offer, but all it did was make her stomach flutter more.

Yanking the bow from her hair, she determinedly brushed out the braid and smoothed it into a ponytail. She had to pull herself together and not allow Gabriel's teasing to fluster her. It dawned on her as she fluffed up her bangs in the mirror that Calvin and Chad teased each other incessantly. If Gabriel's sisters had all left home, wouldn't he miss having someone to tease? Since he had made it abundantly clear he was only being neighbourly, then his teasing could only be brotherly. She sighed deeply and went into the living room. So why didn't she feel relieved that Gabriel was only treating her like a kid sister?

"Mom, can Gabriel stay for lunch?" Calvin shouted as he came running up the cottage steps.

Susannah went to the screen door. "Perhaps we should permit Mr. Desjarlais to get back to his farm and his own chores," she suggested, certain Gabriel could hear their conversation.

"But, Mom, we already invited him and he said to ask you first, but it's okay with him!" Chad hollered breathlessly as he ran up behind his older brother.

Susannah could not think of a polite way to refuse. It really was the least she could do after his hours of arduous work. Her main concern, however, was not so much enduring more of his barbs, but the fact that he would likely discover her culinary deficiency. Her lunch repertoire was restricted to tinned soups and sandwiches. Suppers were only a slight improvement with the addition of tossed salads and anything that appeared on the grocery store shelves as a prepackaged mix.

In the end he did stay, eating his soup without complaint or comment. Calvin and Chad, thrilled to have male company, devoted themselves exclusively to Gabriel. They showed off their rock collections, bug collections, their martial arts skills, and they talked incessantly.

Following lunch, Gabriel returned to the logs, while Susannah and the boys organized them into a pile.

"So what did you do before you came to Lee River?" Gabriel asked when they stopped for a glass of lemonade. "You hardly seem the outdoorsy type." He made a slight grimace after his first sip but said nothing.

"I was a banker, like my husband. Actually I was a Branch Manager and preparing for a promotion to an executive position." Her first attempt at home-made lemonade was proving to be unbearably tart and Susannah set her glass aside, unable to finish it. She noticed Gabriel continued to take small sips from his glass and she considered offering to replace it with a cola. But then why pass up an opportunity for revenge? she thought to herself and bit back a triumphant grin.

"So you must be good with numbers?"

"Yes, I suppose. Banking seemed to come natural to me. I was working on a degree in Business Administration, part-time, before Steven died."

"What on earth brought you out here?"

"I lost my sense of purpose when I lost Steven. I'm not so sure I've found it again." She reached for his empty glass, and her wedding rings glistened brilliantly in the sun. "I spent a summer here with a school friend when I was fourteen. I've always had such fond memories of the place."

Gabriel raised an incredulous eyebrow. "You based the monumental decision to quit banking, mid-career, and throw yourself into a completely foreign environment on a single idyllic childhood memory?"

"I was in my teens," she snapped, "and I will adapt. You're just sore I ended up with this place instead of your mother!"

He laughed before stooping down to retrieve his axe. "I'm far from sore about it, Susannah." He raised the axe high above his head and slammed it into a log.

Susannah stared after him for a moment before returning to the task of piling wood. What had he meant? He was probably just trying to tell her he bore no ill will over losing the cottage to her. Hadn't his hard work already proved that? And what did she care what he meant anyway?

"Calvin and Chad tell me that you won't let them swim at your dock," Gabriel said after they had shared a long silence.

"I'm worried about leeches. I think I'd pass out if they ever got one on them."

Gabriel laughed. "Well, it seems a shame for them

to live on a river and not do any swimming. How about I take you all out in my boat tomorrow?"

"Gabriel, I really think you've put yourself out for us more than enough already."

"We could do some fishing too. They say they've never been fishing before."

Susannah wavered. The boys would love a day of fishing and swimming, but could she risk another day in Gabriel's company with the turmoil he seemed to cause her? She looked down towards the dock where her sons, having long since tired of work, were playing beside Gabriel's boat, and she knew instantly why Gabriel had suggested a boat ride.

"I think they already did a little fishing today."

Gabriel chuckled. "I'm afraid you're right, but I haven't been out fishing for a while myself. It would be an excuse to go."

"Don't you have farming to do at some point?" she asked, offering him an opportunity to bow out.

He flashed her a winning smile. "You just take care of lunch; I'll worry about my farm."

Susannah shrugged. "Well, I suppose it would be nice ..."

"So say yes then. I haven't had a day off in months."

Susannah couldn't resist the gentle coaxing in his eyes. "Well, I suppose you deserve a break after chopping all my wood." She smiled softly. "What time will you pick us up?"

"I'll be by first thing in the morning, which means I should get some farming done." He thrust the axe deep into a log and gave it a tug to make sure the boys could not pull it out.

Susannah nodded and escorted him to the dock. Calvin and Chad pounced gleefully on Gabriel when she announced they were going fishing the next day.

"Why are you doing all this for us, Gabriel?" she inquired, narrowing her eyes in suspicion as she untied the boat for him.

He was standing in the boat and raised his hands in a gesture of surrender and grinned. "I'm just trying to be neighbourly."

Susannah placed a finger on her chin. "And I suppose you take Bert fishing and swimming too?"

"Well, he does look damn good in a bathing suit!"

Susannah could not help but laugh. She passed him the freed rope and watched his eyes grow serious. "You're still wearing your rings."

Habitually, her fingers found the rings and commenced toying with them. "They have the advantage of discouraging uninvited attention." Seeing the question in his eyes, she added slowly, "I'm not ready to remove them."

He nodded, and Susannah wondered if she'd imagined the disappointment in his eyes, and then all her thoughts were drowned out by the roar of the motor as it fired up. Gabriel turned to wave at Calvin and Chad who were playing on the woodpile at the top of the hill. Susannah stood on the dock, watching the boat recede and feeling a new pang of loneliness.

Four

The next morning Calvin and Chad burst in on their mother, hoping to expedite her rising. Susannah had already been awake for sometime, but pretended to be sleeping when her sons pounced on top of her.

"C'mon, Mom, let's go fishing!" Chad urged as he pulled the covers past her head.

"Wake up, Mom! Gabriel's gonna be here soon!" Calvin piped in while digging under the covers to tickle her.

Susannah curled into a ball and yawned. "Guys, I don't think we should go. I'm really much too tired to get up this early."

"Aw, Mom! We have to go!" the boys wailed.

Susannah feigned another yawn and slowly stretched her arms, then lunged for Chad, straddled his legs and yelled, "Tickle Torture!"

Shrieking a war cry, Calvin jumped onto Susannah's back and pried her off of Chad, who immediately flung himself on top of her, screaming, "I've got her." With flailing arms and legs, Susannah prevailed, knocking the boys to the floor. They ran screaming from the bedroom and out the cottage door with Susannah in hot pursuit. She hurdled the coffee table, flew out the door and down the steps and ran headlong into Gabriel Desjarlais. The impact knocked the wind from Susannah as they crashed to the ground.

From beneath her, Gabriel was all smiles. "I had envisioned a more tender reunion, but your enthusiasm was a nice touch."

Susannah struggled to regain her breath, and her wits, aware that his arms held her fast. She was also aware that her skimpy silk nightie was hiked up past her hips, and goodness only knew where the rest of it was.

"I'm only taking you fishing, Susannah. What would happen on a real date?"

Susannah snapped, "Would you please get off of me?"

"Shouldn't I be asking you that?" His hands began to caress her back.

The rapid pounding of Susannah's heart accelerated to a roar in her ears. She struggled to maintain her breath but her words came out in gasps. "Don't flatter yourself, it's just that my nightie's all askew."

Gabriel burst out laughing. "I'm devastated. Here I'd thought you'd fallen for me."

"Gabriel, would you be serious? This is a problem."

"For who?"

"Gabriel!"

"Oh all right, I'll close my eyes."

"I don't trust you," she spat as she clamped a hand over his eyes and sat up, hastily arranging her nightie before jumping to her feet.

"Can I open them now?"

"You better!" Susannah giggled as Calvin and Chad hollered "Hiee yahhh!" and vaulted from their hiding places in the bushes before pouncing on Gabriel.

He raised his arms to his head in mock defence

against a volley of punches. "I can see you boys learned your social graces from your mother. You folks sure have an unusual way of greeting guests."

"Take care of him, boys," Susannah ordered with a chuckle. "I'm going to get dressed."

She was still chuckling to herself as she slid the strap of her one-piece bathing suit over her shoulders. She could hear the ongoing horseplay in the backyard and Gabriel making as much noise as the boys. Just like Steven used to. She sat on the bed and watched them through the window. Was she betraying Steven in some way? She had lain awake most of the night, wanting to spend another day with Gabriel, yet afraid to and not knowing why.

She sat up with a sigh. Most likely she was torturing herself for no reason. Maybe he was just being neighbourly. Maybe he simply wanted to be a big brother to all three of them now that his sisters were gone.

The thought was sobering.

She remembered his hands caressing her back and her tummy did a somersault. A brother indeed! That was no brotherly caress. Then what was it? He always seemed so determined to prove her attraction to him. Was he just trying to rankle her for the fun of it, or was there more to it? Just how immune was Mr. Desjarlais?

She tore off the bathing suit, replacing it with a bright pink string bikini. She examined herself in the mirror and blushed. She supposed the strategic bits of cloth could be considered a bathing suit. It was no wonder Steven had never allowed her to wear it in public, although he had certainly enjoyed the view from their secluded condominium balcony.

She shivered and covered the bikini with an oversized T-shirt, hoping her courage wouldn't fail when the time came. She tied her hair with a pink bow, chortling as she visualized the look on Gabriel's face. He would accuse her of attempting to seduce him, but she'd casually declare she was accustomed to wearing it, and she'd point out that since his only interest in her was as a neighbour, what difference did it make what she wore?

"Neighbourly indeed," she snorted as she packed a hat and sunglasses into a beach bag. She giggled as she headed to the kitchen just as her youngest son burst through the cottage door.

"Mom, hurry up!"

"Chad, I just have to pack the cooler and I'll be right out."

"Okay, but hurry! We'll be waiting down by the boat." He scurried out the door, letting it slam behind him. Susannah laughed to herself, knowing he was worried he might have missed a moment of unsurpassed fun with Gabriel and Calvin.

She lowered the cooler to the floor near the refrigerator and began filling it with the elaborate finger sandwiches and the fruit and vegetable platter she had laboured over the night before. She admired one last plate of ribbon sandwiches, thankful she had humored Steven's mother who had insisted that since Susannah's culinary skills were limited to sandwiches, she could at least learn to assist Steven with entertaining by making fancy ones.

However, she had never learned to bake. And as thankful as she was for Ada Semchuk's cookies, a tin of which she now placed in the cooler, she couldn't help but question the woman's motive in continually presenting her with fresh cookies. It seemed to be an excuse to worm out each and every tidbit of gossip regarding Gabriel Desjarlais. Ada's success in this endeavour was primarily due to

Calvin and Chad's boundless chatter rather than Susannah's own confessions.

Yesterday, Gabriel had scarcely left when Ada's bulking form had emerged from the bushes. "Well I see you won't be needing Bert to help with that wood. I saw you trying and said to him he should help, but he had that stroke, you know, so it's not a good idea." She had prattled on as she presented Susannah with a plate of cookies. "These here are raisin oatmeal. Gabriel's favourite. It's the only recipe I never gave his mother. I told her I had to have something special to give that hard working lad whenever he found time to visit with my boys." She nudged Susannah with an elbow. "But, you could probably convince me to give you the recipe someday. I won't be around forever."

"Gabriel's taking us fishing!" Chad informed Ada with sparkling eyes. Calvin took the plate of cookies from Ada and carefully carried them into the cottage. "We're going to save them for Gabriel," he explained solemnly.

"He's taking you fishing tomorrow?" Ada continued after Susannah's nod. "I must say he's spending more time away from that farm of his than I've ever known him to. Hardly ever took time off before. Not during berry season anyway."

She leaned over and winked. "Honey, you're gonna have to learn to cook. A man who works as hard as Gabriel won't survive long on love and sandwiches!"

Seeing the bewilderment on Susannah's face, she patted her arm. "Your boys told me you can't cook. But I'll tell you what. You let old Ada here teach you and you'll have that Gabriel eating right out of your hand." She broke into a hearty cackle and then waved at Bert who was calling from the bushes at the edge of Susannah's lawn. "That man is utterly helpless without me!" She shook her head in exasperation. "I hope he goes first. I'd get along fine, but he'd be lost by himself." She headed towards her cottage, adding before she disappeared into the bush, "Mind you, it was a terrible scare for me when he got sick."

"I'm sure it was," Susannah had called back sympathetically, realizing that it had been her first and only opportunity to open her mouth since Ada's arrival.

Susannah chuckled, knowing today Ada would be sitting on pins and needles, obsessing over what might develop during the fishing trip and driving poor old Bert crazy.

"It's just a fishing trip," Susannah insisted, packing beverages and ice into the cooler. She snapped the lid shut and attempted to lift the cooler but could barely move it.

"Calvin, could you come here a minute please?" she called from the screen door. "Take the other handle, honey," she instructed when he came bounding through the door a moment later, "and help Mommy drag this to the dock."

"Let's get Gabriel to do it, Mom. He's strong!"

"I know he's strong, Calvin, but let's try to do this ourselves, shall we?"

Taking hold of the handles, they pulled the cooler along the floor and out the door. Calvin was more of a hindrance than a help, but she had no wish to injure his pride so she permitted him to continue holding the other handle even though he tended to pull in the opposite direction. She could hear Gabriel whistling "Oh Susannah" down at the dock. He broke off when he saw her struggling with the cooler and jogged up the hill. Calvin, relieved of his burden, trotted down to the boat where Chad was examining a fishing rod.

"Here, let me take that." Gabriel took the cooler from her with one easy swing of his arms. "Whoa, what have you got in here? This is heavy!"

Susannah gave him a sideways glance. "Well, Mrs. Semchuk does claim you are a big man with an appetite to match. Besides, I filled it with rocks to give you an opportunity to impress me with your male strength."

Gabriel let out a laugh and set down the cooler. "Why, Susannah James, I do believe you are flirting with me!"

"I am not!" she sputtered, turning red and stamping a foot. "I simply wanted to demonstrate that I'm not as impressed with you as you believe I am."

"Is that right?"

She glared up at him. "It certainly is."

He grinned. "You forget, Susannah, I raised four sisters."

"And so that makes you an expert on women?"

"Just about," he said, picking up the cooler and heading down the path to the boat.

Susannah glared at his back and followed grudgingly, wishing she were an expert on single men.

When they reached the dock, Susannah was surprised to find a functional aluminum fishing boat in place of the sleek, fibreglass speed boat she was accustomed to seeing. Gabriel helped her and the boys aboard and passed out life jackets.

"There's usually good fishing by Coca-Cola Falls. The swimming's nice there too," he informed them as he started the engine and directed the boat out of the small bay which sheltered Susannah's cottage.

"Coca-Cola Falls! Yumm!" Chad squealed.

"It's not made of coke, dummy!" his brother snorted.

"That's right, it's not," Gabriel interjected gently, not wanting to encourage a row. "But it does look like cola because of the iron in the water."

"Neat!" the boys exclaimed, forgetting their animosity.

Susannah lay against the blankets and extra life jackets at the bow and peered across the river. "So where is your farm?"

"That log cabin straight across from us. The farm itself begins just past the trees at the top of the hill." He pointed to a sprawling home whose sole claim to the appellation "log cabin" lay in its having been partially constructed out of rough-hewn logs.

"You're directly across from us?" Susannah sat up to assess the degree of privacy at her own cabin.

"Yes, and the main reason your place would have been ideal for my mother. She could have signalled me if necessary." He grinned knowingly. "But she would have still been able to maintain a degree of privacy."

Susannah folded her arms across her chest. "Well I refuse to feel guilty. My sons are much happier since coming here and so am I."

His dark eyes twinkled. "It must be all those raspberries."

She licked her lips thoughtfully. "I'm more inclined to believe it's Mrs. Semchuk's cookies."

"Yeah! And she made your favourite kind, Gabriel. And we saved them for you!" Calvin piped in.

Chad touched Gabriel's arm and stared gravely up at him. "We didn't even eat one."

Gabriel ruffed the boy's hair and winked at Susannah. "Well, we'll have to make certain we eat them very soon, won't we?"

Except for the small wake their boat left behind, the river was a calm, glassy sheen, as it was every morning. Susannah marvelled that a river could be so ideal for swimming any time of day and wide enough to host an abundance of water sports while still permitting a sense of wilderness and isolation.

Besides the soft hum of the motor, the lapping of the water against the boat, and the odd cawing of a crow, the only other sounds on the lake were those made by the boys as they fired a bombardment of questions at Gabriel. Susannah smiled at the wonder in their voices and the way their eyes lit up as they occasionally reached over the side of the boat to splash their hands in the cool water.

Susannah closed her eyes, savouring the morning sun and the fresh, dew-filled air. How long had it been since she had felt so content? Not since before Steven's death. Was Gabriel a contributing factor, or was it simply the solitude and peace of their new home?

She opened her eyes to study Gabriel. To her surprise he had been studying her. Their eyes met.

Susannah turned away and searched for words with which to dispel the intimacy between them. None came, so instead she pretended to be engrossed with the various cottages which dotted the shoreline.

"I think yours is the nicest place I've seen so far," she commented at length, glad for something to say. "It's also the largest."

"My father built it for my mother while they were still engaged. The farm has been in my family for generations." He smiled. "I think he wanted to impress his prospective bride so he tore down the old homestead and built her the largest home in the area. My mother was partial to log cabins, so he incorporated modern amenities with country charm."

"If the inside is anything at all like the outside, it must be very beautiful."

"You'll have to come see for yourself sometime," he said with a wink.

Susannah wasn't sure how to respond and was grateful when Chad whined that he was hungry. From the soiled dishes in the kitchen sink, she knew the boys had helped themselves to breakfast and suspected Chad's hunger was directly related to the cookies in the cooler.

Gabriel turned the boat into a small bay which was fed by a frothy stream of dark, almost black, sparkling water. It truly did look like cola bubbling over the rocks into the river. "How about if us men get the fishing rods ready while your Mom finds those cookies you saved for me?"

Calvin and Chad readily agreed, their eyes, however, riveted on the cooler even as Gabriel dropped an anchor over the side of the boat.

"Mrs. Semchuk sure makes good cookies, eh Gabriel?" Chad sputtered through a mouthful a moment later.

"You bet!" Gabriel concurred, munching on the last of his cookie as he continued to check the line on Calvin's rod.

"Mom doesn't make cookies," Calvin said dourly, his voice tinged with resentment. "Sometimes my dad did, but Mom doesn't know how to make anything unless it comes in a can."

Susannah froze, the cookie which she had been nibbling on still at her mouth. She made an attempt to swallow, but her mouth had turned horribly dry. She refused to look at Gabriel although she could feel his eyes upon her.

He spoke softly. "Everyone has at least one special

talent, Calvin."

"What do you mean?"

"Well, Mrs. Semchuk bakes wonderful cookies, but she probably couldn't be a bank manager like your mom."

Calvin was silent for a moment. "You mean like how I'm good at Nintendo, and Chad is good at soccer?"

"Exactly," Gabriel replied with a pat on Calvin's back.

Susannah kept her eyes averted. She was relieved Gabriel hadn't laughed at her and was angry with herself for having cared what he thought in the first place. This was the nineties. Lots of women couldn't cook.

Gabriel finished preparing Calvin's fishing rod and set it aside.

"Is that for Chad?" Calvin asked as Gabriel reached for the next rod.

"Sure is."

"I'll do it."

"Pardon me?"

Calvin clenched his teeth. "I'll do it."

Gabriel stared at him, astonished. "You'll do it?"

"That's what I said, didn't I?"

"Calvin! Mind your manners," Susannah admonished, but Gabriel raised a hand.

"Okay. I'll fix your mother's and you can watch and prepare Chad's at the same time."

Calvin nodded as Gabriel handed over Chad's rod. Gabriel began to whistle "Oh Susannah" as he casually threaded a line through Susannah's rod, patiently demonstrating how it should be done. Calvin's head was bent in serious devotion to the task.

"My dad died when I was twelve," Gabriel said in

between whistles. "I guess that's older than you are now, but I was still only a young boy."

Calvin paused and looked intently at Gabriel. "My four sisters were just little, one of them was even a baby." Chad crawled over and wriggled his way onto Gabriel's lap. Gabriel draped an arm around him and continued, "I was scared, being the only man in the house, but I knew my sisters needed someone to look after them."

Susannah pretended oblivion, sensing a purely male intimacy at the other end of the boat, but couldn't prevent the tears from sliding down her cheeks.

"Sometimes, when the work got real hard, I got angry at my dad for dying, but mostly I just missed him so much I didn't think I could stand it. When I thought of him up in heaven and looking down on me, I decided that I wanted him to be proud of how hard I tried." He bent down to look Calvin in the eye. "I think your daddy is very proud of how well you take care of your brother and your mom."

Affecting preoccupation with the fishing rod, Calvin surreptitiously wiped tears from his face with an arm. Gabriel said no more, instead attaching a hook at the end of Susannah's line and watching Calvin follow suit.

"Thank you," Susannah said as she wiped at the tears on her own face before reaching for the rod Gabriel held out to her. He held onto it for a moment, forcing Susannah to meet his eyes. In their dark depths she saw unspoken comfort. He touched her arm briefly, then turned his attention to the boys.

"All right. It's time to get down to some serious fishing!" he announced as he stood up. "Watch closely 'cause I'm gonna ask each of you to do this in a moment." He swung the rod behind him and released the clip on the reel as he cast, the line flying through the air and over the water before plunging into it. After the line had dangled in the water a moment, he reeled it back in and then cast out again. He instructed each of the boys to do the same and continued giving pointers until they could do it on their own.

Susannah kept a watchful eye on the hooks, worried one might accidentally embed itself into the tender skin of one of her sons.

When it was her turn, Gabriel watched with a grin as she half-heartedly swung her rod. "You're going to hook one of us if you're not careful."

She scowled. "That's precisely what I'm worried about."

He took the rod from her and again demonstrated how it should be done. She made another attempt but the line fell limply into the water next to the boat. Gabriel positioned himself behind her and took hold of her casting arm, guiding it through the swing. "Don't release the line just yet; go through it a couple of times first."

Susannah tried but was now more nervous of Gabriel's close proximity than of the hook. He placed his other arm around her waist and held her against him as he swung her arm. She resisted the urge to rest against him. How long had it been since she had been in a man's arms? He smelled of the outdoors, fresh air and the woods.

He stretched back her arm, nuzzled her ear and whispered, "Mosquitoes are attracted to perfume, you know."

Flustered, she jabbed him in the ribs and shoved him away, hissing, "Thank you, Entomologist Desjarlais! I'll remember that."

Gabriel burst into laughter, and Susannah swung

the rod full force. The line shot out several metres and dropped into the water as if it had been propelled by a proficient angler. She stuck out her tongue at Gabriel.

"With the right motivation, I think you could do anything, Susannah," he grinned.

Susannah reeled in her line and expertly cast it again. She beamed. "I think this is an indication of who's likely to catch the most fish."

"It wouldn't surprise me a bit," he chuckled as he cast his own line and sat down.

Accepting the truce, Susannah joined him and the four of them sat for some time, casting and recasting. At times one of their lines would get snagged on a weed, and Gabriel would have to tie a new hook onto a broken line. The boys were unusually quiet, having been warned that noise would scare away the fish. Even when an occasional fish jumped in the water, the boys managed to keep their decibel level to just above a whisper.

"Are you bilingual?" Susannah asked quietly some time later, breaking the blissful silence.

"Yes," Gabriel replied as he tied a hook onto Chad's line.

Susannah nodded and tugged her line.

"You didn't ask what my second language was."

"With a name like Desjarlais, I would presume it's French."

"Actually my French is pretty good, but I speak Polish better."

"Polish?" Susannah echoed, astonished.

"Yes. My mother was born in Warsaw. Her parents were killed during the Second World War, and an uncle managed to bring her over."

"But you are also Metis, are you not?"

"Sure am. Somewhere down my father's family

tree is a beautiful Indian woman and a French fur trader. What about you?"

Susannah laughed. "I haven't got a clue what I would be classified as now. Just Canadian, I guess but –" She broke off with a squeal. "There's something on my line! I can feel it wriggling and pulling!"

"No way!" Calvin cried as he clambered over to her.

Gabriel sat close by and coached her catch. "Pull back and then reel in the slack." Not once did he try to relieve her of her rod while the grappling fish was tugged from the water.

He reached over the side and unhooked it. "It's a pickerel!" he exclaimed as he held it up for her inspection.

"I caught a fish! I caught a fish!" she squealed as she stuck out her tongue at her sons. "And it's the first catch of the day too!"

"I'm gonna catch a bigger one than that!" Chad retorted with disdain.

"Betcha can't catch another one!" Calvin challenged.

"The water will keep it fresh until we get back," Gabriel explained as he attached Susannah's victim to a chain which he hung over the back of the boat.

Susannah leaned over to survey her fish. "Hah! I'll bet you thought I wouldn't catch one!"

He laughed. "Well, sweetheart, I hope you'll be this excited when it comes time to clean it."

She sobered momentarily then shrugged a shoulder, saying pertly, "I don't care. You show me how, and I'll clean them all. They'll likely be all mine anyway."

Gabriel threw back his head with a hearty laugh. "Well just remember, Susannah, you said it, not me."

Susannah ignored his laughter and reached over the boat to inspect her fish once more. How hard could cleaning a fish be?

Five

Susannah slid her knife up the fish's belly and scraped out its entrails. "I'll never eat caviar again!"

She had scaled and cleaned seven fish and had one more to go. Her sons' predictions had been correct in that Chad's did turn out to be the largest, and she did not catch another.

The boys had long since ceased watching her work, having become bored after the second fish and having gone on to assist Gabriel in building a fire.

Prior to this, Gabriel had carefully demonstrated the proper method for cleaning a fish and had then presented her with the knife, saying, "You did say you would clean them all."

"What if I don't do it right?" she had asked, nonplussed.

"Practice makes perfect."

Pride had prevented her from arguing the point, so she had commenced scraping fish scales with a vengeance. "I'd like to scrape him away," she grumbled under her breath, her hands covered in slime.

Upon completion of her task, Susannah marched over to him and dropped the fish at his feet with a triumphant smile. "Done!" she announced and without a backward glance marched up to the cottage to wash her hands.

"Bring out a pan and some butter, and I'll show you how to cook them," Gabriel called out, his voice resonant with amusement.

Susannah took advantage of being inside to change into jeans and a fresh blouse, blushing as she removed her bikini. For all her efforts, she never did find the courage to disrobe in front of Gabriel.

The bikini, however, had not gone without notice; as she had prepared to dive over the side of the boat for a swim, Gabriel had inquired with his usual wide grin, "Aren't you going to remove your T-shirt?"

Susannah had shook her head shyly.

"That's a pity! All morning I've been looking forward to seeing that little string bikini!"

Mortified, she had dove into the water, only to discover when she climbed back into the boat that the drenched, white shirt had become transparent and was clinging like a second skin, exposing the bathing suit in its sparse entirety.

"You may as well have taken it off," Gabriel had told her as he had helped her climb back into the boat, his eyes shining with obvious appreciation.

She glanced at the wet patch of pink now dangling from the bed post and shuddered. What had she been thinking? No doubt Gabriel had thought she was looking for an opportunity to throw herself at him. Her plan had backfired and she should've known better. After all, she had difficulty looking Gabriel in the eye at times, let alone nearly baring herself before him. She should've worn the one-piece and left well enough alone. If Gabriel was as attracted to her as he fancied she was to him, he couldn't hide it forever. Somewhere along the way, he'd slip up and she'd be there to gloat.

She pulled her hair back with a decorative comb and went into the kitchen to unpack the cooler. They had devoured all but a couple of finger sandwiches for lunch, the remainders of which she placed in the fridge, smiling as she recalled Gabriel's praise. Wearing that same smile, she made her way down to the riverbank, carrying on a tray tossed salad, potatoes wrapped in aluminum foil, and a skillet with butter.

"You're just in time," Gabriel declared, poking at red-hot coals and fanning smoke from his face as she set the tray down beside him. He placed the potatoes strategically amongst the coals, then balanced a grill on the surrounding bricks. He set the skillet on top and grinned up at Susannah. "We'll add some butter, and you folks can enjoy your first fish fry."

Susannah watched with a shudder as he placed a fish in the sizzling butter. "Would you chop the head off mine, please? I've had more than enough of looking at dead fish for one day."

He smiled as he complied with her wish. "After the job you did cleaning these fellows, I think you should have them any way you want."

"You mean I did a good job?" she asked, incredulous.

"No, I mean being as they are only partly gutted and only barely scaled, removing their heads can only enhance their appearance."

Susannah's mouth dropped open in dismay. She had been so proud of herself. Why her final fish had even looked as good as the one Gabriel had cleaned.

"I'm kidding!" he laughed. "You can scale my fish anytime."

"Thank you ... I think," Susannah giggled.

After cooking the first pan of fish himself, Gabriel turned the task over to Susannah, who found she enjoyed cooking over an open fire. She removed the fish onto waiting plates. "I feel like one of those pioneer women you read about in historical romance novels. I wonder if any of them started out as city slickers like myself."

Gabriel chuckled. "At the rate you're going, Susannah, you won't be a city slicker for long."

The meal was wonderful. Susannah couldn't remember when she had enjoyed fish as much. Calvin and Chad, not subject to the squeamishness their mother suffered, were quite willing to eat not only fish with their heads attached, but the heads also. Gabriel and Susannah laughingly discouraged their enthusiasm in that regard.

Shortly after dinner, as they lounged in the cedar lawn chairs and watched the setting sun display a glorious hue of oranges and reds, Gabriel announced, to a chorus of "Aw's," that it was time for him to leave.

"Thank you for a wonderful day, Gabriel," Susannah said sincerely as she watched him untie his boat from the dock.

"The pleasure was mine, Susannah," he stated simply. He bent over to pull the cord on the motor, then seeming to change his mind, turned to face her. "I won't be able to stop by for a few days." He sounded apologetic. "It's the height of raspberry season."

Susannah fought the disappointment rising within her. "You've already been far kinder than we've deserved. We never expected you to do so much for us in the first place."

"I certainly think you're worth the trouble, Susannah," he said softly before finally pulling the cord. She watched him pull away from the dock, then she turned and started up the hill, sighing deeply as his familiar whistle faded into the night.

Six

Five days later, Susannah and the boys still had not heard from Gabriel. She was both surprised and disturbed to discover that she missed him. Perhaps as much as Calvin and Chad did. Several times a day they voiced the very questions whirling in her mind: where was he and would he ever come back?

She gave them the same pep talk that she gave herself. He was, when you got right down to it, a comparative stranger and under no obligation to them whatsoever. He was a very busy man with a life of his own, and it was extremely generous of him to have spent as much time with them, his new neighbours, as he had. And as much as they enjoyed his visits, they shouldn't expect them. Yet every morning, she could only watch helplessly as her sons ran down to the edge of the dock to listen for his boat.

She tried to keep them occupied with a barrage of activities ranging from bike rides and hikes and trips into town for soft ice cream, but it did little to curb this morning vigil. And when an afternoon rain earlier in the week forced the boys indoors to entertain themselves, Susannah found that despite herself she was keeping a silent vigil of her own.

Thus had begun her determination to keep herself

occupied by cleaning and organizing the cabin.
Although she could manage the basics, there was
much that she didn't know, and Ada Semchuk had
spent a good part of the last two mornings imparting
knowledge and muscle. Susannah had worked
tirelessly in the evenings after the boys were in bed,
and as she watched them now skipping rocks over
the water, she realized that for all her efforts, her
mind was no less on Gabriel than theirs.

"What d'ya say, Susannah," Ada practically
shouted, startling Susannah as she elbowed her way
through the bushes and into Susannah's yard, "now
that I've shown you how to wash and polish them
hardwood floors, would you like me to teach you to
cook?"

"Ada," Susannah laughed, "you've been so
helpful; but I couldn't possibly take more of your
time!"

"Rubbish! I've got nothing but time. And besides,
it would keep me out of old Bert's hair." Ada
laughed heartily as she showed herself into
Susannah's cottage and helped herself to coffee. She
poured Susannah a fresh cup before sitting down.
"This being retired is hard on both of us. Seems we
never have enough to do. We're hard working folks
who don't know how to sit still." She went on,
barely pausing for breath. "We tried one of them old
folks places in the city, but I just didn't enjoy doing
crafts and playing cards all the time. And Bert! Well
he was the most miserable man you'd ever wanna
meet. Forty-five years of marriage and I was ready
for a divorce."

She got up and opened Susannah's cookie tin
which was now always full. Placing a plate of
cookies in front of Susannah, she sat down and
continued, "You haven't been eating much I notice.

These will fatten you up. Anyways, Gabriel stops by to visit us one day when he was in Winnipeg on business and says there's a cottage for sale right across the river from our old farm. Well old Bert's face lit up, and we moved out here two months later. Been here five years now," Ada stated firmly. "So now what do you want to learn to make first? Gabriel's favourite is perogies."

Susannah opened her mouth and promptly closed it.

"Of course he likes cabbage rolls too, but we could start with perogies." Ada folded her arms resolutely across her generous chest. "We'll start right now. I don't got nothing else to do."

She stood up, her hulking form filling Susannah's tiny kitchen. "Raspberry season will soon be over. Next time he comes over you'll be able to serve him your homemade perogies."

"Ada, I'm not sure there will be a next time that Gabriel visits us," Susannah replied, sounding more despondent than she intended. "But I do enjoy perogies, so I wouldn't mind learning to make them."

Ada clucked her tongue. "If I don't know Gabriel Desjarlais, then I don't know my own sons either – he'll be back."

The two women spent the afternoon preparing perogies, the expert patiently helping the novice fold small circles of dough over a whipped potato and cheese filling. When complete, the perogies were coated in flour and stored in the freezer for later use, but Susannah reserved a few which she later boiled in water, then sauteed with onions and butter and served for supper.

"Mom, you made these?" Calvin asked with disbelief as he smothered his perogies with sour cream.

Susannah glowed with pride as she sat down for supper with her sons. "I sure did and I'm going to learn how to make other things too."

"Wow!" an awe-struck Chad exclaimed between mouthfuls.

Susannah had to agree as she ate, unable to decide which was more satisfying – the perogies themselves or the praise of her sons.

She thought about satisfaction later that night as she sat around the campfire with her sons and tried to make some sense of the chaotic flickering flames. She ignored her sons bickering about who had first dibs on the best marshmallow-roasting spot, and closed her eyes, welcoming the heat on her face, wishing it could rekindle her hopes that Gabriel would return. Failing that, if she could at least pretend to go on as if it didn't matter, then perhaps her boys, whose growing antagonism toward each other was most likely related to Gabriel's absence, would eventually forget about Gabriel.

She laughed to herself and poked at a smouldering log, knowing it would be some time before the impact of Gabriel's absence fizzled out. She cast a worried glance at her youngest son, then winced as his marshmallow plummeted into the fire. His ensuing cries could be recognized by any mother as those of a little boy who should be in bed.

"You're not doing it right, stupid," Calvin sneered.

"That's because you're hogging the fire," Chad shoved his brother.

"That's enough!" Susannah warned. "Chad, I'm going to get more marshmallows, then Mommy will help you roast one. After that it's off to bed, the both of you!"

"You promised we could stay up late!" Calvin

protested while Chad wailed that he only got to eat two roasted marshmallows.

"It's way past your bedtime," Susannah countered. "There'll be other opportunities to roast marshmallows. I don't want any fighting while I'm gone, or this will be the last time we roast marshmallows. Got that?" Both boys nodded sulkily, snarling at each other with their eyes.

She left them poking their sticks into the fire and hoped they wouldn't kill each other. This day will be over in a few minutes, she told herself as she trekked up the path toward the cottage. The faint sound of a boat had her stopping and straining to hear. She chided herself for hoping it was Gabriel. Neighbour or not, he wouldn't be dropping in unannounced at this time of night.

She continued up the path, yawning along the way and wishing she hadn't promised Chad another marshmallow. Stepping inside the cottage, she was instantly tempted to call the boys in. But a promise was a promise. She grabbed the package of marshmallows from the kitchen table and headed back out the door.

She'd only gone a few steps when the sound of her sons giggling caught her attention. Perhaps Gabriel had shown up. Maybe he'd seen their campfire from across the river and decided it wasn't too late to drop by.

Feeling foolish for such wishful thinking, she realized by some act of God her boys must have made up. She breathed a sigh of relief and quickened her pace down the path. As the darkness gave way to firelight, she stopped abruptly, her heart twisting in terror as she beheld them laughing and playing with a bear cub.

They were hand-feeding the tiny cub the remains

of Calvin's roasted marshmallow. Susannah stood for a moment, breathless and paralyzed. If the mother bear, who was sure to be close by, discovered them, she would tear them to pieces.

She raced down the path, screaming so sharply the boys momentarily froze while the cub bounded off into the bush. "Leave that bear alone and get back to the cottage this instant!"

"Mom, you scared it away!" Calvin cried, stepping into the bush.

"Don't you dare go after that bear!" Susannah screeched, yanking him back. She grabbed both boys by their shirt collars and forced them up the path.

"When I tell you boys to do something," she barked, "I expect you to obey. Now walk as fast as you can up to the cottage. Walk," she yelled in vain as they broke into a run. She ran behind, not wanting them out of arms' reach, all the while praying that the mother bear didn't come charging out of the bush.

When the cottage screen door was within her grasp, she yanked it open and pushed her sons inside, tripping in behind them and accidentally knocking them all to the floor.

"Mom!" Chad whimpered from beneath his brother as they clambered to their feet. "You're a meanie."

"I'm not being mean, now get ready for bed and I'll explain later. Go on," she commanded, waving them off, and watching their small bodies shuffle out of sight.

She sighed against the door and closed her eyes, indulging in several deep calming breaths, only to find herself screaming as a loud pounding scarcely preceded the door pushing open.

"Is everything all right in there?" Gabriel boomed

as he forced his way through the door.

Susannah was so relieved she nearly burst into tears. She quickly turned from his searching gaze, thankful her sons were bounding from their bedrooms and racing across the living room with loud whoops. They flung themselves at him.

"Whoa!" Gabriel laughed as he embraced them. "I see the greeting rituals around here haven't changed much."

"Guess what we saw tonight?" Calvin blurted.

"A bear!" Chad interrupted.

"Yeah, a cute cuddly baby bear!" Calvin added.

"And it really likes roasted marshmallows," Chad piped in. "It's little tongue licked my finger when I gave the marshmallow to him." He held up the finger to Gabriel.

"It was just the most exciting thing!" Calvin beamed, his eyes dancing.

Gabriel cast an uneasy look to Susannah who was busy dabbing at tears. "And then what happened," he asked the boys cautiously as he pulled out a chair and sat down.

Calvin's face fell. "Well, then Mom –" his lips trembled, "came screaming down the hill and ruined it all! She chased it off into the bush and we'll never find it again!" He began to cry openly, and Chad followed suit. Gabriel hoisted each of them onto his lap.

Tears streaming down her own face, Susannah looked on helplessly while her sons sobbed into Gabriel's chest. "They're very tired."

"I know," he whispered and stroked Calvin's hair. "You know what, son, I would've done the same as your mother."

Calvin sat up, rubbing his eyes, while his brother remained nestled against Gabriel's chest, his eyes growing heavier with each breath. "Whyyeeee?"

Gabriel let out an uneasy breath, and glanced up at Susannah, who smiled her assent.

"Well," he began slowly, "as hard as it may be to imagine, a baby bear is very dangerous."

"Is not!" Calvin refuted. "A big bear would be dangerous but not a baby ..."

"But that's the problem, Calvin. A baby bear is never alone. There is always a bigger bear close by. Usually its mother."

"Well, we didn't see no mother bear."

"You may not have seen one, but I can guarantee you she was not far away. And that's what makes a baby bear so dangerous." When it was apparent that Calvin could not make the connection, Gabriel continued. "Was your mother angry when she discovered you boys playing with the baby bear?" Calvin nodded. "She wasn't angry with you, she was afraid that the bear might hurt you. And you know what else?" Calvin shook his head, his fingers in his mouth. "The mommy bear would have been afraid you were going to hurt her baby."

"We were just playing. We weren't going to hurt it! Honest!"

"I know that, but mommy bear wouldn't have known that. And so she would've tried to hurt you. Now do you understand, Calvin, why your mother chased the bear away?"

Nibbling on a fingernail, Calvin nodded then scrambled off Gabriel's lap to his mother. Susannah hugged him tightly. "I love you, Mommy," he whimpered.

"And I love you more, sweetheart!" She kissed his cheek, rocking him slowly. She stared down at Gabriel, and Chad, who was now snoring in Gabriel's arms. "I think it's time somebody got to bed, don't you, sweetie?" she whispered to Calvin who merely yawned in reply.

"I'll take care of this one," Gabriel said, scooping Chad into his arms and heading off towards Chad's bedroom while Susannah delivered Calvin to his. He was asleep before she had finished putting his pyjamas on, and from the darkness of the hallway, Susannah watched his peaceful form. She stepped back as she closed the door and stifled a scream when she bumped into Gabriel. He steadied her, his hands on her waist as she turned around. His eyes locked on hers.

"How's momma bear?" he asked softly.

Susannah blinked back tears. The need to throw herself into his arms was overwhelming. "Okay," she managed.

"You're frazzled," he countered, brushing wisps of hair from her face. An errant tear meandered down her face and Gabriel caught it with a fingertip.

Susannah kept her eyes averted, terrified he would see the need in them.

"It's all right, Susannah," he whispered. "You don't have to be strong."

Even as he spoke, Susannah exploded into tears and clung to him as his arms wrapped around her. "I was so scared, Gabriel. What am I doing out here? I'm in way over my head. I should've just stayed in the city ... but I was useless there too."

"I thought you were a bank manager," he whispered into her hair.

"I was," she lamented. "But that was about the only thing I did. Steven took care of everything."

He stroked her hair. "I can see a man wanting to take care of you, Susannah," he murmured.

She relaxed against him, breathing in his power and strength, absently skimming her fingers over the borders of his shirt pocket. "I should have done more, but Steven made it too easy and now I can't even feed my own children without being taught how."

Gabriel chuckled and raised her chin. "Susannah, I'll bet whatever Ada Semchuk has taught you, you already excel at." He caressed her cheek, and she shivered with wonder. His hand exuded the same power that emanated from his body, yet the touch on her skin was tender. It made her yearn for the full strength of his touch. She pressed her cheek into his hand.

"Perogies," she whispered. "She taught me how to make perogies."

He grinned and traced the outline of her lips with a finger, causing them to part with an escaping sigh. "I'd say for what you've been through, you're doing better than many other women would have." He laughed softly. "I'd even bet you'd have mastered splitting those logs if someone had shown you how."

She smiled at him, her tears having subsided to the residual droplets resting on her lashes. He planted a brotherly kiss on her forehead. His lips lingered, then began to forge a slow path towards her eyes, which she closed in response. No longer content with her eyes, his lips traced a fiery route down her cheeks. Susannah's breathing had all but ceased when his lips kissed the outside corners of hers. Her moan was guttural when she opened her mouth to receive his kiss. And her disappointment acute when he pushed her away.

He turned his dark head aside and cursed himself. "I'm sorry, Susannah. I always hated it when I thought some guy was trying to take advantage of one of my sisters."

She stared up at him in shock. *I'm not your sister!*

she wanted to scream. She choked back fresh tears and watched him head for the door.

"I have to go, Susannah," he said, his hand on the knob.

She would not ... could not look at him.

"Susannah," he repeated.

She stood stiffly, her eyes fixed on the door behind him. He rubbed his dark chin which was shadowed with a day's growth of bristles. And then he was gone.

Seven

Sleep eluded Susannah. Bears intermingled with flashes of Gabriel haunted her dreams. She tossed and turned, searching for an exorcism of the images, but neither phantom would release its grip. At long last, just as the sun began to paint the sky with touches of light, her lids closed in repose.

She had scarcely been asleep when a pounding on the cottage door barged in on her slumber. Irritated, she tossed on her housecoat and went to discover who had interrupted her hard-gained rest. Gabriel stood at the door.

Susannah withheld a greeting, the sting of the previous night's humiliation still fresh.

Not waiting to be invited in, he took her arm and pulled her into the kitchen. "I wanted you to know that you don't have to worry about those bears anymore," he said, keeping his voice low.

"Why not?" Calvin demanded, having quietly wandered into the kitchen.

Gabriel hesitated. "Because me and some other farmers made sure they went far away."

"You scared them away?"

Gabriel ran a hand through his hair and sighed. "I guess you could say that."

Calvin pondered this a moment. "Well, I suppose

that's okay. I was sort of hoping to see that baby again, but you know, Chad would probably be real scared if he knew the mother was still around and all, and I'd really hate for us – I mean – Chad to be too scared to go out and play."

"There's nothing to be afraid of now," Gabriel reassured. "But living in the country, bears sometimes do wander nearby. If you see one just back away from it slowly, and whatever you do, don't run. It'll probably be more scared than you."

Susannah dropped an arm around her son. "Why don't you go wake your brother and get dressed?" She gave him a gentle push and he darted off towards the bedrooms, yelling Chad's name and spouting news about the bear.

Gabriel took a seat at the kitchen table, leaning his head against the wall. Dark circles haunted his eyes and lines of fatigue were drawn across his forehead. He sighed heavily as he rubbed the thick stubble which was threatening to become a full-fledged beard.

Reluctantly, Susannah's heart softened. "You look exhausted."

He raised his tired eyes. "Yeah, we've been tracking those bears all night. I originally stopped by last night just to warn you about them. We had to shoot the mother," he moaned.

"Oh, Gabriel ... I am so sorry," she said and sat down with him.

"We had no choice. We weren't able to scare her off, and with that cub, well we just couldn't risk allowing her to stay."

Susannah reached for his hand. "What happened to the cub?"

He held her eyes for a moment and cupped her hand in both of his. "My brother-in-law took it.

Someone from the Department of Natural Resources will be out to fetch it today."

"Will it be put in a zoo?"

"No, he'll be trained to be self-sufficient and then released back into the wild."

"I wish the boys could see him."

"So do I, but contact with humans has to be kept at a minimum. If he becomes too comfortable around them not only would he be less likely to survive in the wilderness, but he could present a real danger to humans." He was softly stroking her hand. She could feel the calluses on his palms, a testament to the labour he was accustomed to. His fingers brushed over her wedding rings.

Nervous of the intimacy between them, Susannah pulled back her hand and made a pretence of brushing the hair from her face. "Would you like to stay for breakfast? I can cook eggs, you know," she said with a laugh.

He grinned. "I won't be risking my life?"

She jumped up to open the refrigerator. "There's only one way to find out." Pulling out bacon and eggs and placing them on the counter, she indicated the back porch with a nod. "The newspaper should be here by now."

Gabriel went to retrieve the paper and Susannah sighed. Perhaps the best way to deal with last night's kissing fiasco was not at all. They'd both been tired and emotionally spent. There was nothing more to it. And to eliminate any doubt, he'd made it quite clear that she wasn't his type. Well, neither are you mine, she snorted to herself as she lay strips of bacon in the hot skillet. The sting she was feeling was merely wounded pride. Still, it irked her that he seemed to enjoy sending her mixed messages.

She snuck a glance at him and watched as Calvin

entered the kitchen and pushed his way onto Gabriel's lap. She frowned. She really ought to discourage her sons from becoming too attached to him. A moment later, as if summoned by the aroma of sizzling bacon and brewing coffee, a sleepy Chad, still in pyjamas, joined his brother on Gabriel's lap, leaving the man no alternative but to cease reading. She bit her lip worriedly. He looked like a father with his sons.

Chad rested his head on Gabriel's shoulder and stared up with adoration. "Can you take us fishing again sometime?"

"Chad!" Susannah remonstrated. "That is very bad manners."

Gabriel came to the boy's defence with a chuckle. "How's a fellow supposed to get what he wants if he doesn't ask?"

She glared at him before turning her back to scrape butter across a piece of toast. What was that supposed to mean? She continued manipulating the knife across the toast with such ferocity that she scraped off the crisp browning. "I suppose that's quite true," she said at last, tartly. "It helps when you know exactly what it is the other person wants. It makes things less confusing."

"Ouch!" Gabriel declared with an exaggerated wince.

She made no reply but kept her back to him as she broke eggs into the skillet. The loud crackle as they scorched in the pan did not obscure the challenge in his voice as he spoke across the kitchen. "If there is anything that you want, Susannah, all you have to do is ask."

Shivers ran up her spine. What did he mean by that? She certainly knew what it sounded like. If she wanted him, all she had to do was say so? Was it really that simple? Did she want him?

"That means we can go fishing again!" Calvin whooped, taking Gabriel completely at his word.

Gabriel roared with laughter and playfully boxed the boy's ears. "I'll tell you what. If it's nice, I'll take you to Pinawa Dam for a swim on my next day off."

"Yippee!" The boys exclaimed as they hurried to their chairs to receive the plates of bacon and eggs Susannah placed on the table.

She was returning with Gabriel's and was pondering plausible excuses for not going when Ada Semchuk burst through the door.

"Mornin'," her voice boomed. She halted when she spied Gabriel reaching for his breakfast.

Susannah realized how the situation appeared – she in her nightie and housecoat and serving him breakfast. Aghast, she warded off a blush and opened her mouth, but Gabriel stood up, his eyes dancing with mirth.

"Can I get you a chair, Ada? Susannah's just made a fresh pot of coffee."

Susannah cringed. He was playing the gracious host and making it sound as if the two of them had been drinking coffee together since the crack of dawn.

"Uh ... I'd love a cup ... thanks," Ada replied hesitantly. Strangely silent, she dropped herself into the chair Gabriel pulled out for her.

Susannah poured her neighbour a coffee and sat down, debating whether it would be better to explain Gabriel's presence at the breakfast table or keep quiet. Given Ada's remarkable curiosity, it was possible she was already aware Gabriel had only just arrived. If Susannah made any attempt to explain, it might put ideas in the woman's head. And Ada had enough ideas of her own without help from

Susannah.

"We were just about to eat breakfast," Gabriel cheerfully stated the obvious.

"Oh you just go right ahead and don't bother about me," Ada said with a wave of her massive arms, their folds of fat quaking. She swilled her coffee and stared at Gabriel, dangling an unasked question in her eyes. "You're here bright and early."

"Yes ... very early."

Susannah stabbed her egg with her fork.

Ada gulped her coffee, draining the cup. "I didn't hear your boat. Did you come by the road?"

Gabriel pushed egg onto his fork with a knife and paused. "No I didn't come by the road, my boat's down at the dock."

"Gabriel was here last night!"

Susannah jumped at Calvin's excited testimony.

"Yeah, an' he tucked me into bed!" Chad added.

Susannah swallowed her coffee with a choke and had to excuse herself while she went to the sink to cough. Damn him! She glared at him over top of Ada's grey head. He flashed his white teeth and shrugged his shoulders, insinuating helplessness.

Ada lifted her mug to receive the refill Gabriel offered and stated emphatically, "Well I can see I won't be able to just pop in anymore." She helped herself to several spoonfuls of sugar. "And I guess I'll have to start knocking too." She sipped her coffee, lost in thought. "You young folks do things different than in my day."

"Ada, I think ..." Susannah began as she sat down.

Ada cut her short with a loud guffaw. "Well, well! I told you perogies would be the way to Gabriel's heart!"

The blush Susannah had been fending off since Ada's arrival finally scorched her cheeks. Furious, she tossed aside her napkin and pushed back her chair. Forming her face into a counterfeit smile, she modulated her voice to deceptive sweetness. "Ada, Gabriel has been out all night stalking a bear. When he arrived at our door this morning, he was utterly exhausted, so I offered him breakfast. I can't have you thinking there's more to it than that. He's far too much a gentleman." She couldn't prevent the acidity from creeping into her voice as she tossed a smug smile in his direction. "Why he has never so much as kissed me."

The disappointment on Ada's face was readily apparent as she digested this information. Her face broke out in a broad grin as a new thought occurred to her. "Aha! Things are more serious than I realized." She turned to nudge Gabriel with a voluminous elbow. "Not even kissed her, eh? This one's special, is she?"

She lifted her huge frame from the chair. "Well this I gotta tell old Bert. C'mon back to Auntie Ada's boys and help old Bert pull up weeds, and I might make some fudge."

She scooted Calvin and Chad out the door and called back to Susannah with a cackle, "Gabriel Desjarlais isn't exactly known for his restraint when it comes to chasing a woman. Looks like I'll be going to a wedding real soon!"

The cackles continued until she was out of sight. Susannah rolled her eyes heavenward and gave her head a despairing shake. "I love that woman dearly, but she does have some strange ideas."

Gabriel folded his arms across his chest and stared at her. "Oh, I don't know about that. I think she made the same assumption dozens of others would have made if they'd come upon you serving me breakfast in your pyjamas."

She sneered at him. "Yes, and you certainly enjoyed yourself, didn't you? Why didn't you tell her you hadn't spent the night when it was perfectly obvious that is what she thought?"

He chuckled. "According to Ada I have a reputation to maintain, and besides, she's not as observant as she thinks."

"Oh really? Why is that?"

"If I had spent the night, believe me, you wouldn't be wearing a nightie under that housecoat."

Involuntarily, her hand clutched at the opening of her housecoat. "You're just trying to make me blush," she accused as a bright crimson stole across her face.

He laughed. "And according to Ada, you're trying to tempt me to the altar with perogies!"

Susannah sputtered, "You know I'm really regretting having felt sorry for you. In fact, I'm feeling sorry that bear didn't get you before you got it."

She stomped off to her room, slamming out the echo of his laugh with the door. Angrily pulling on denim shorts and a tank top, she paused in the mirror for a brief examination. Seeing her auburn hair in disarray, she scooped it into a loose knot atop her head, not bothering to correct wavy tendrils which slipped loose and curled about the nape of her neck.

She put her hand on the doorknob and stopped. She couldn't face him yet. Her face was still flushed and she didn't feel prepared to dodge further taunts. The nerve of him! Using her to maintain his reputation as a rake.

She studied her reflection in the mirror and bit her lower lip. A tremor ran through her. Was he as virile as Ada inferred? It excited her to think he might be. She had never been with any other man but Steven. What would making love with Gabriel be like? Her body went warm as she envisioned him kissing her and touching her.

The heat was chased away by an invading sadness. Making love with Gabriel was obviously something she would never experience. He had made that absolutely clear last night. And as for Ada's gibberish about a wedding ... well that's precisely what it was, gibberish!

Dejected, she returned to the kitchen. Gabriel was gone. It struck her as odd that he hadn't said anything before leaving, but she had been in a huff, so perhaps he had decided to avoid her altogether.

She stared at the mess of waiting dishes. The kitchen seemed empty without Gabriel. She was sorely tempted to postpone cleaning up and go lie in the sun instead but knew she'd be even less motivated later. She held back a groan as she filled the sink with soap and water, realizing Ada had been right about doing a little bit of cleaning every day to keep things from piling up. That sort of self-discipline Susannah had yet to master, but as she filled the sink with soap and water, she vowed she would.

Half an hour later the kitchen sparkled brightly as Susannah tossed the dish cloth into the sink. She put a load of laundry in the wash, folded and put away yesterday's load, and made a mental note that the boys were to clean their rooms before they could watch any television today. She quickly made her bed and tidied her own room then sighed with satisfaction at her clean cottage. Now she could soak up the sun with a clear conscience.

She crossed to the living room to retrieve her novel from the coffee table, and stopped, startled by the sight of Gabriel stretched out on her sofa, sound asleep. She smiled. It seemed so right that he was there.

Taking a blanket from the linen closet, she gently covered him. Bending over to tuck the blanket behind him, her eyes wandered over his dark, rugged face. He looked peaceful. She whispered, "What am I going to do about you, Gabriel Desjarlais?" Pausing to lift a strand of hair from his brow she added softly, "The woman who ends up with you is going to be very happy indeed."

Picking up the novel she tiptoed to the door, pulling it softly closed behind her.

"Thank you, Susannah," Gabriel called out sleepily through the open window by the sofa.

Her feet froze on the small verandah. Had he just awoke and discovered the blanket, or had he been awake all along? Her stomach lurched, and then she sighed with resignation. If he had heard her, she was bound to find out sooner or later because he wouldn't pass up an opportunity to tease her.

Gabriel slept most of the afternoon. Susannah passed the time lying on the lawn in a patch of sun which peeped through the trees. A soothing breeze caressed her skin while the pages of the novel unfolded. Eventually the book slipped from her hands, and she fell into a restful drowse.

Sometime later, when she opened her eyes, Calvin and Chad were diving from Gabriel's fishing boat which was out on the river. She sat up on an elbow and peered at them from underneath a hand, shading her eyes from the late afternoon sun.

Gabriel must have discovered she was awake because he waved in her direction, and the boys scrambled into the boat. Soon the sound of the engine could be heard as Susannah strolled to the dock.

He greeted her with a smile. She caught the rope he tossed and tied it to the dock. Calvin and Chad's attempts to assist Gabriel succeeded only in causing the boat to bump hard against the protective tires which lined the edge of the dock.

"Careful guys," Gabriel admonished. "I don't mind with this old tub, but next time I'll have my ski boat."

Calvin climbed out. "Hey Mom! Gabriel says for sure we can go to Pinawa Dam on Saturday if it's okay with you." He tugged at Susannah's arm. "So can we go?"

Chad quickly joined the appeal by tugging on her other arm. Gabriel came to her rescue by ordering them up to the cottage for dry clothes, saying he and their mother would discuss it. "I hope you don't object to my taking them for a swim without your permission."

She was relieved he had changed the topic. "No, not at all. I feel badly you were left to baby-sit while I napped."

"It's the least I could do after unceremoniously helping myself to your sofa."

Susannah laughed. "I suppose we're even then."

They had been walking towards the cottage. He stopped and turned to her. "Is that why you won't commit yourself to the dam?"

"What do you mean?"

"I can't help but notice you haven't said yes or no."

Her grey eyes grew serious. "Gabriel, you do too much for us already. I don't want you to feel that we expect things from you. I don't want us to become a burden."

He grasped her by the shoulder. "I wouldn't object to your depending on me."

"It's Calvin and Chad," she confessed, avoiding his eyes. "I'm worried they're becoming too attached to you."

"They're great little guys. I'm partial to them too."

Susannah persisted. "Gabriel, some day you're going to find a new life for yourself. What then?"

His eyes were dark with sincerity. "I promise you, Susannah, I will walk out of your lives only when you ask me to."

She searched his face, wanting to trust him.

"I promise," he repeated. He draped an arm over her shoulder and gave her a winning smile. "Now how about a day at the dam?"

Her smile was shy. "When you put it like that, how can I refuse?"

"Good!" he stated, releasing her. He glanced hesitantly towards the cottage then back towards his boat. "I should be getting back. Things are pretty busy at the farm right now. I won't be able to get over here before Saturday." He started towards the boat.

Susannah's heart sank. Today was Monday. "That is precisely why I'm upset," she began, as she followed him to the dock. "The boys will come out to the dock every morning and watch for you. It will take all I can do to distract them! Gabriel, I tell them not to; I try to keep them busy, but nothing works short of locking them in their rooms."

Gabriel climbed into the boat, untied the rope and sat down. His face broke into a smile. "Well, I guess I'll just have to make sure I get here before Saturday."

"You don't have to do that."

"But I will." He started the engine and gave her a crooked grin. "So, Susannah, do you come to the dock every morning and watch for me too?"

She snorted. "Of course I don't."

He laughed. "That's too bad. I thought maybe you did since you're so sure the woman who ends up with me is going to be one happy lady."

Susannah wished the dock would collapse and swallow her, but all she could do was stare, engulfed in embarrassment, as he drove away, the faint strains of his trademark whistle rising above the hum of the engine.

Eight

He was true to his word. Although sometimes stopping only long enough to bring them a basket of berries, he managed to visit once a day. For Calvin and Chad, his visits were the highlight of the day. Susannah also found her day incomplete without the appearance of Gabriel.

She occupied the time with more of Ada's cooking lessons and yard care tips from Bert. She discovered she enjoyed working outside. The cooking was coming along nicely, but gardening was proving to be a natural talent.

Bert had shown her which of the vegetation in her flower beds were weeds and which were not. It was too late in the season to plant much, but she did manage to sow a few rows of lettuce, radishes and marigolds.

Calvin and Chad on the other hand, were not quite as easily entertained, and Susannah found herself giving them small chores to occupy their time. School was going to be a welcome diversion, but it was now only late July, and an entire month of vacation was yet to come.

She herself was not sure what she would do once the boys returned to school, but there was no immediate hurry to find a job. Steven's insurance policies had left them well provided for, and as Bert had assured her, preparing the cottage for winter would involve a fair amount of work. But not enough to last past November, she thought to herself. Then what would she do? Winters could be long and lonely, especially in a relatively isolated place like Lee River.

She was musing over this dilemma at her kitchen table, when her boys burst through the cottage door, the youngest yelling, "Mom, Bert's taking us clubbing!"

"Golfing! Stupid!" Calvin corrected, yelling.

The door had no sooner slammed shut behind them as they raced back out when Ada barged in.

"I got a hankerin' for blueberry pie!" She dropped several plastic pails and a picnic basket onto the table. "Bert's gotta go to Pine Falls this morning and we thought the boys might wanna come along. Later they could bang a few balls around the golf course, so I thought you and I could do some blueberry picking."

Susannah smiled affectionately. It seemed everything had already been decided and she suspected Bert and the boys were already in his car, waiting to go, if in fact they hadn't already gone. She chuckled inwardly and asked, "And where might your secret blueberry patch be? No one ever divulges the location of their favourite patch!"

Ada found a mug in Susannah's cupboard and drained the last of the coffee into it. "There's no secret about this patch. It's on my old farm, and every summer Gabriel lets me pick my fill." She swilled the coffee in her mug, downed in it one gulp and grimaced. "You could have warned me it was stone cold."

Susannah giggled. When had she had a chance to

say anything? "I'll go put some jeans on," she said as she wandered off toward her bedroom. When she came out, Ada was already packing the trunk of Susannah's car. The boys were indeed already in Bert's car, and so excited that when he drove off, they barely bothered to holler a goodbye or even wave. It was wonderful to see them so happy.

"So, Gabriel bought your farm?" Susannah asked as she opened her car door.

"Yep. And we never even had to put it up for sale! The day Bert started talking retirement, Gabriel started talking buying. Of course, we grew grain, not berries, so he leases out most of the land to a neighbour, but he did convert some of it to berries and expanded his own farm."

"What about your house?"

Ada snorted as she squeezed herself into the passenger seat beside Susannah. "I suppose he could have sold it off as a cottage to some city folks, but he uses it in the summers to house the university students he hires to harvest berries."

Along the way Ada pointed out several fields. "Those there are some of Gabriel's strawberry fields – the season's over already, so he'll be harvesting raspberries about now but those fields are farther out."

Susannah gazed out over acres of tender strawberry plants arranged in tidy rows and sectioned off by spruce trees which provided protection from the harsh prairie winds that blew down from the Arctic or across the west from the Rocky Mountains. She smiled. The endless miles of flat prairie land held a beauty all its own. It gave one a feeling that the sky never ended. And things didn't sneak up on prairie dwellers. There was really no place to hide. Even the weather could not arrive unexpectedly.

"That's Gabriel's house," Ada said, pointing. "We could stop and visit his mother, Mila, but she's in Winnipeg this week."

Susannah glanced sideways, feigning disinterest. Not that there was much to see anyway, as only a small portion of the cedar-shingled roof was visible through the trees. She was relieved to hear Gabriel's mother was away. Routinely coping with Ada's misconceptions of a romance between herself and Gabriel was tribulation enough without having to endure scrutiny from Mrs. Desjarlais as well.

Ada directed Susannah down a road leading to an old two-storey farmhouse. "There's the old homestead!"

Susannah parked in the centre of the yard and surveyed it as she climbed out. Apart from a badly needed coat of paint for the wood siding, the house appeared to be well maintained. An old barn and shed, also in need of fresh paint, sat quietly on the opposite side of the yard near a row of tall and aged poplar trees which provided the requisite windbreak. Although what appeared to have once been Ada's vegetable garden was now wildly overgrown with weeds, the remainder of the yard was neatly mowed. And despite the clothesline weighed down with jeans and T-shirts which she assumed belonged to the summer help, a loneliness permeated what had once been the Semchuk farm, as if it were waiting for someone. She thought of her condo back in Winnipeg, and how the life of a new family would by now have filled it and erased all traces of Steven. She wiped a tear away.

As Ada lugged her huge form out of the car, Susannah asked, "Wasn't it difficult to leave all your memories behind?"

Relieving Susannah of the picnic basket, Ada

shrugged. "Sure, this was our home and old Bert was born in this house, but farming is hard work. I never knew any other way of life. Mind you, I never wanted any other life, but with farming you're at the mercy of the weather. We just got too old and tired. It was a comfort to close the door behind us, knowing Gabriel would take care of it." She patted Susannah's arm tenderly. "Besides, I took my memories with me. I didn't leave nothin' behind. And neither did you."

Susannah contemplated Ada's simple approach to life as she followed her down to the river and the precious berry patch. Would she ever be able to take life in its stride the way Ada seemed to?

The blueberries were in little clusters nestled along the river's edge. Susannah had never seen them in their natural habitat before. They had always arrived on her table via the supermarket.

Reaching down, she plucked a handful from the greenery which sat low to the ground. The berries were like smoky blue pearls which turned a dark navy when touched. She popped some into her mouth, savouring their tangy sweet flavour.

"You're as bad as my boys!" Ada cackled in between mouthfuls of her own. "They always ate more than they picked and complained of sore tummies later."

They laughed and settled into picking, crouching alongside one another, filling their pails, sometimes chatting and at other times lapsing into meditative silences. Ada talked of her years on the farm, and as Susannah listened she found herself envying the life Ada had lived.

The bank, Steven and the city – it was all beginning to feel distant, as if that life had belonged to someone else. Here among the berries she felt at peace. Lately, it seemed she felt at peace whenever she was working with her hands near the soil.

When Bert had first encouraged her to at least remove the weeds from the flower beds around her cottage, she had balked, terrified of unearthing worms or other creepy crawlies, but the first time she had tugged loose a weed and witnessed an earthworm hurriedly tunneling back into the safety and darkness of the soil, she had been amazed at its strength and speed. And she had sympathized with its desperation to find shelter. It was rather like how she had felt after Steven's death.

After that first encounter, working the soil with her bare hands was less frightening, and she became curious about the world beneath her feet and how things drew life from it. It was as if she, too, were drawing life from it.

She began avidly reading gardening books and magazines and continually pestered either Bert or Gabriel with questions. Gabriel would chuckle and tease, saying Bert had unleashed a monster, but he seemed pleased with her interest. Once, while she was dragging him around the yard, showing off her efforts and badgering him with questions, she caught him wearing a secretive smile.

"What's so amusing?" she had asked.

He grinned. "You look happy. Like a little girl."

Indignant at being reduced to a helpless child who needed his fraternal guidance, Susannah pulled herself up to face him. "In case you haven't noticed, I am a fully grown and capable woman with two sons and a career. Not everyone is born a farmer!"

Gabriel had exploded with laughter. "Susannah, if there is only one thing I have noticed, it is that you are indeed every inch a woman." His eyes had caressed her as they travelled the length of her body.

He had been grinning, but his eyes had remained gentle and serious and seemed to search for something in hers. "Maybe there's more farmer in you than you realize."

Even thinking about it now as she picked blueberries, her skin burned beneath the memory of his gaze. She shivered involuntarily. Maybe he was right. She did seem to have a way with the soil. Perhaps that was the sort of work she should look into, rather than banking. There were a few nurseries in the area. One of them might hire her. And maybe one day she would have her own nursery. It was something to think about.

She was still thinking about it late that afternoon when she emerged from the bushes that divided the Semchuks' cottage from hers. Gabriel was waiting at her back porch. He had repaired a loose board on her steps and was putting away his tools.

"Well, well, what have you got there?" he asked, peering into the bulging pails of berries she was carrying. "I see you've been out with Ada." He grinned mischievously. "Is she going to teach you how to make pie? Did she mention that blueberry is my favourite?"

Susannah fought back a blush. Ada had indeed told her it was his favourite, and Susannah had intended to make him one, simply as a gesture of gratitude for his kindness.

She raised a defiant chin. "I was going to make you one, but now that it's clear you'd mistake it for a seduction ploy, I'll eat it all myself. You see, it's my favourite pie too."

"Well I guess I shouldn't have opened my big mouth," he laughed. "Seems I've talked myself right out of a pie." He snapped the lid closed on his tool box and gave her a boyish grin. "So what's new in the horticultural department?"

Susannah studied his face for signs of teasing, then smiled shyly. "There's something in the rose bed, and I was hoping you could identify it. It's probably a weed, but I'm not sure."

As he followed her to the roses, she decided not to mention her idea of finding work in a nursery. He'd probably set about securing her a job somewhere. And she already owed him far too much. As much as she appreciated the daily effort he made to see her and the boys, the likelihood of his eventual exit from their lives continued to gnaw at her. Would Gabriel be as willing and able to devote his time to them when a woman finally claimed his love? Perhaps he wouldn't mean to break his promise, but ...

Moments later, as she watched his truck pull away from her lot, she wondered what sort of woman he would love. Obviously nothing like herself. Probably she would be sleek and fashionable like his ski boat, a sharp contrast to Susannah's unassuming winsomeness.

Ada, however, persistently maintained that Susannah was what Gabriel needed, and never missed an opportunity to discuss the matter, usually during their daily cooking class. They had taken to working in Ada's kitchen as it was larger and more accommodating to two women, particularly when one of them was of Ada's dimension.

"I see Gabriel Desjarlais stopped by again last night," Ada would say and then stare expectantly at Susannah.

After Susannah's sparse recap of his visit, Ada would snort, "He sure does got it bad for you, don't he?"

"He's simply being kind," Susannah's defence was the same each time. "He knows how lonely the boys are for male companionship."

Ada would chortle. "It's you he's comin' to see!"

Susannah would protest that she and Gabriel were merely casual friends, at which point Ada would cackle loudly just like she was doing now. She dumped a cup of sugar into a mixing bowl and began stirring vigorously. "Friends is a good place to start, honey, but I haven't known that boy for all his life and not known when he's got a woman on his mind, and you, Susannah, are that woman."

"I'm hardly Gabriel's type," Susannah replied dryly. "You said yourself that one of his girlfriends was a Toronto fashion model."

"Yep! Met her there on business. She was at the farm once. Too skinny if you ask me."

"There, you see? He even brought her home to meet his family."

Ada put her hands on her hips and shook a wooden spoon at Susannah. "Well he never married her, did he? He didn't marry none of them, and the reason is they weren't his type, and he knew it. Gabriel's always known what he wants, and he wants you. It's as plain as the nose on my face."

These conversations with Ada invariably brought Susannah back to the same question. Why did Gabriel bother with her and her sons? The only sense she could make of it was that he missed his sisters, but his tendency to flirt didn't fit the puzzle. One thing was certain – she needed a clear definition of her relationship with Gabriel, not only for her own sanity, but for Calvin and Chad's as well. Having lost their father, they needed stability, not to be dangling in limbo with Gabriel.

And the only way to guarantee them stability was to take control and relegate Gabriel to the status of big brother and not allow herself to be affected by his capricious flirting.

She was determined in her resolve to the point of instructing her sons to look upon him as an uncle.

"But who's gonna be the Auntie then?" Chad asked that night as she tucked him into bed.

"What do you mean, sweetie?"

"If Gabriel is our uncle, then who's the Auntie?"

Susannah hugged him. "Gabriel doesn't have a wife yet, but someday he will. When that happens he probably won't be able to take you swimming and fishing anymore because he'll have his own little boys to do that with."

"Won't he love us anymore?"

"Of course he'll still love you, Chad. It's just that when a person has children to take care of, it's harder to find time to be with other people." She stroked his cheek and planted a kiss on his forehead. "When you're a daddy you'll live somewhere else and won't visit me very much."

"You mean I won't live with you anymore?"

Susannah shook her head.

He pouted with determination. "Well then I'm never gonna grow up."

Susannah laughed as she turned off the light. "Every grown-up said that when they were little."

Closing the door behind her, she searched the living room for her novel, finding it on the coffee table underneath the boys' comic books.

Sighing, she stretched out on the sofa and opened the book. Evenings were difficult. The time alone after the boys were in bed left her vacant. She and Steven used to reserve the evenings for each other. It was the time of day when they caught up on one another and renewed themselves.

Lately, instead of reminiscing about Steven, her mind strayed across the river. What did Gabriel do in the evening? Did he work late on the farm and fall exhausted into bed? Did he read? Watch television?

A knock sounded at the screen door, startling her out of her musing. Setting the novel on the sofa, she cautiously approached the door.

"The Northern Lights are putting on quite a show," Gabriel said in an undertone through the screen.

She waved him in. "I've just put the boys to bed."

Rather than entering, he reached through the open door and drew her out. A dampened evening welcomed her. She drew in a long breath. Truly, there was nothing so fresh as country air on a summer's eve.

He led her off the porch and onto the grass, which was damp with dew. "I know you always have them in bed at ten o'clock sharp."

Susannah glanced at him ruefully. "I'm not that regimented, am I?"

He laughed. "Consistency is not a bad thing, you know."

"Well it's the banker in me ..."

He silenced her with a hand on her mouth. "Look!"

"It's beautiful," she murmured as her eyes beheld the dreamy filaments of light dancing in the heavens.

They strolled down to the dock where their view was unencumbered by trees and foliage. The night was alive with a celestial celebration of light which pulsated across the horizon. Streams of light swelled to brilliance and then waned to a mist, mingling with one another in an exotic dance of colour.

Gabriel retrieved a blanket from his boat.

"Here lie on this," he said as he shook it out, allowing it to drop softly onto the grass. "This way we won't get stiff necks from looking up, and our backsides won't get soaked with dew."

Susannah remained standing and eyed the blanket apprehensively. "So long as all we're going to do is watch the lights."

Gabriel, already comfortably stretched out on the blanket with his head underneath his arms, looked up innocently. "Why, what else could we do?"

"You know perfectly well what I'm referring to."

He reached up and pulled her down. "I think I do, but you could explain anyway just to make sure we're not misunderstanding one another."

He wrapped his arms around her, his lips only a breath away. Dark eyes held her captive. At that moment, more than anything else in the world, she wanted his kiss. What if she just put her mouth over his?

A replay of the last time their lips nearly touched flashed across her mind. She wasn't a complete fool. A man telling her once that he wasn't interested was more than enough.

"I'll risk being misunderstood," she said flatly as she pushed away and lay on her back beside him.

He gave her a mischievous grin. "Have it your way."

They watched the display of lights in silence, Susannah becoming so enthralled that she ceased to notice how close their bodies were or when she had come to rest her head upon his shoulder.

"They're so much more spectacular than in the city," she breathed. "They fill the entire sky."

"My great-grandfather used to call them down to us. He said anyone with a drop of Native blood could do it, if they called upon the Great Spirit."

Susannah giggled. "What did he do? Some sort of chant?"

"No, he used to make a low whistle ... like this ..." He began to whistle tunelessly.

Susannah sat up halfway and laughed outright. "You can't whistle the Northern Lights down from the sky. They're protons and radioactivity and reflections of the sun and stuff!"

"Shh!" He coaxed her head back down to his shoulder. "Watch."

He whistled quietly while she stared up at the sky. The lights pranced above her. Their glow filled the firmament from beyond the highest star down to the crest of the forest. They rose and fell, falling nearer and nearer until she was drawn up with them. She became the light, rising and glowing and flowing.

Unexpectedly frightened by the experience, Susannah gave a sharp laugh, breaking the spell. She sat up and poked Gabriel with a finger. "It's a natural phenomenon. They're absolutely beautiful, but you didn't make them happen."

"Think what you like," Gabriel replied with a secret smile which expanded to a grin. "I've noticed you haven't been wearing perfume lately."

"You said it attracted mosquitoes."

He nodded, still grinning. "That's true, but I didn't say it repelled men."

Susannah was grateful for the cloak of night which hid her blush. Was he teasing or flirting? What would he say if she started wearing perfume again? He'd tease her no doubt.

She rolled onto her stomach, resting on her elbows, and looked at him from a safer distance. "So how much Metis blood do you have anyway?"

"I have no idea, but a fair bit I would imagine. An aunt is working on the family tree, but I haven't seen her for years."

"Did your family keep much of the culture?"

Gabriel turned onto his stomach beside her. "I've only recently been rediscovering my Metis heritage.

After my father's death, it was nearly lost. And with my mother being Polish, it's difficult to decide what my culture really is, but I feel a strong pull to the Metis. When I'm with my Polish relatives, I can be a part of them, but when I'm with my father's family, it's where I belong."

"Maybe who you are is everything mixed together," Susannah suggested. "Goodness knows, my family certainly is. I couldn't even begin to untangle the cultural hodgepodge of my family tree. I've got everything in me from Scottish and Dutch to plain old Yankee."

"I'd like my children to know their roots. It's important to know who you are."

Her stomach lurched. Was he speaking hypothetically, or did he have the children of a specific woman in mind? She sat up. "It's getting late. Calvin and Chad are not prone to sleeping in, so my day starts early."

Gabriel stretched and yawned deeply. "Mine too." He picked up the blanket. "I'll walk you to your door."

When they reached the cottage, Susannah no longer wanted to go in. She leaned against the screen door, prolonging his stay. "Thank you for thinking of me. It was nice to watch the lights. I don't go outside much at night."

"Still nervous of bears?"

"A bit."

He caught a strand of hair which had strayed from her braid. "Don't be. Nothing's going to hurt you out here."

"I'm not so sure about that, Gabriel."

He released her hair. His hand brushed her cheek and then her neck. He brought his mouth down to hers.

She closed her eyes and received his kiss with sweet relief. His lips were soft, warm and inviting. His kiss deepened. Feelings Susannah thought had died with Steven awakened from deep within. A familiar hunger but for a new man. His arms engulfed her, submerging them both into a storm that knew no calm. She could taste the fury of it and needed to be consumed. He drove her into the door, crushing her against himself and robbing her of her gasp for air as he seized her by the hair and continued to raid her mouth.

He breathed her name, his breath hot against her mouth, his heart thundering against hers. "If I don't leave now ..."

"Leave?" she moaned as his mouth found hers again.

"You'd only hate me in the morning," his ragged whisper caressed her ear.

"No," Susannah murmured as she drew his face back to her.

But he pulled away gently, cupping her face in his hands. His eyes locked with hers. "Susannah, I don't want it like this."

Tears of humiliation sprang to her eyes. How could she have allowed this to happen again? Rage followed humiliation. He had deliberately led her on. What was she? Some sort of toy he played with so long as it was on his terms?

Before she could muster the nerve to slap him, he had taken hold of her left hand. He fingered her rings. "Do you?"

Susannah yanked her hand away, her eyes filling fast with tears. "Just go," she sputtered, shoving him away and drawing her arms to her chest, suddenly cold. He reached for her, but she twisted away and stared at the ground, refusing to look at him.

"Susannah," he whispered, "please don't cry."

She burst into tears and spun around, fumbling her way into the cottage. He didn't follow her, and she hated herself for wishing he had.

Nine

Susannah and the boys were ready and waiting when Gabriel coasted up to the dock the following morning at ten o'clock sharp. She had contemplated sending the boys down to tell him they couldn't go because she was ill, but knew she would have had a mutiny on her hands. She had contemplated being sullen and rude, but in the end chose to carry on as if nothing had happened. And apart from the grave look he gave her as he tossed the boys a rope, Gabriel seemed to be doing the same.

Chad's eyes shone brightly as he secured the rope to the dock. "Does this boat water-ski?"

"You bet!" Gabriel chuckled, pointing to the shiny metal bar at the back of the boat before hoisting Chad into the boat. "But not today because I didn't bring skis." He reached for Chad and then took the towels from Susannah, locking her eyes with his as he did.

Susannah blinked and shielded her eyes as if the morning sun was too much for them. Gabriel stood a little too close, and his hand at her waist lingered a little too long as he helped her into the boat. The gentle squeeze of her shoulders as he slipped a life jacket over them had Susannah fighting a blush at the memory of having practically begged him to sleep with her.

She supposed she should thank him, she thought as she took her seat next to his at the front of the boat. He had been right. Her first thought upon waking had been how glad she was to find the place beside her empty, which was ironic, considering that every other morning for the past year and a half, she had hated that empty bed.

Sneaking a glance at his unmitigated masculine build as he sat down and started the engine, she decided it would have been a pleasure, but she was not the sort to make love out of sheer loneliness, no matter how much she might enjoy it. She needed commitment, and Gabriel had never indicated anything more than a mild interest. And that for the meantime only, until the woman of his dreams materialized.

She drummed her fingers on the side of the boat and frowned. Things seemed to have a way of getting out of control whenever Gabriel Desjarlais was around. She laughed inwardly at her resolve the previous day to treat him like a brother. It had lasted all of about 10 minutes – until he had shown up at her door. She watched as he propelled the speed boat along, the shore diminishing before her eyes, and knew she was too far gone to alter the course they were on now. She only hoped she didn't make a big fool of herself before he found Ms. Perfect.

Not daring to dwell on where he might lead her or when it might end, she turned her gaze from him to her boys. They were sitting in the back of the boat, complying with great difficulty to Gabriel's stern command to remain seated at all times. Thrilled screeches erupted from them as Gabriel slowed the boat to manoeuvre through a twisting, rocky passage beneath a bridge. Their wake sloshed up against the rocks, causing the boat to sway menacingly in its narrow course.

Susannah put a nervous hand against the dash and leaned forward, anticipating release from the make-shift tunnel.

"I've been through here hundreds of times," Gabriel reassured and removed her hand, intertwining it in his. "Trust me, Susannah," he whispered, and when Susannah met his penetrating gaze it was clear he was referring to much more than his boating skills.

What was he saying? That he'd never hurt her? Never take advantage of her. He'd so much as admitted last night he could only give her a temporary relationship. Hadn't he?

The other side of the bridge gave way to a calm channel edged with tall prairie grasses. There were occasional settlements of cottages, but most of the bordering land appeared to be farm acreage.

She was relieved when he released her hand and announced they were mere moments from their destination before turning off the motor and standing up.

He motioned for her to switch places with him. "It's your turn."

"My turn?"

He gave her a broad grin. "Sure! Wouldn't you like to drive?"

She eyed the steering wheel warily. "I've never driven a boat before."

"It's easier than driving a car."

Calvin leaned forward, careful to keep his bottom to the seat. "Hey Mom! If you learned to drive a boat, maybe we could get one."

Chad jumped up, forgetting his bottom. "Mom's gonna drive the boat?"

Panic rising, Susannah looked at Gabriel but spoke to the boys. "No. Mom is definitely not going to drive the boat."

"It's very simple," Gabriel assured. "It's clear sailing from here to the dam. No rocks. No islands and wide enough to accommodate three boats."

"No ... thank you."

"You don't think you can do it?"

"Of course I can do it."

"So why don't you then?"

"Because I just don't want to."

His voice was deep and silky. "You aren't afraid, are you?"

"Not at all."

"You don't trust me then, is that it?"

"Of course I trust you."

Warm dark eyes coaxed her frightened grey ones. "Then trust me, Susannah. Drive the boat. I think you'll be glad you did."

Susannah felt sick. Telling a man like Gabriel that you trusted him was as good as telling him you loved him. She felt like she was being tricked. She meant she respected his judgement. She meant she regarded him as honest. But now, after having thrown herself at him the night before, he would assume she was in love with him. His teasing would be relentless.

She cringed at the thought. He'd pick his moment, as he usually did, waiting until she was completely off guard, and then he'd hit her square in the face with a taunt.

"All right!" she hissed. "I'll drive your damn boat."

Calvin and Chad let out a "whoop" and abandoned all attempts to remain seated.

"Gabriel!" Calvin chortled. "Mom said the 'D' word!"

Gabriel laughed and wagged a finger at her as they exchanged places. "She sure did!"

Susannah glared at him as she placed shaking hands on the steering wheel. "I hope you've got lots of insurance, and if I drive us to the bottom of the river and we all die, I hope you know it will be all your fault."

"Don't worry, you'll do fine." He laughed. "Okay! The first thing is to simply turn the key. It should start right away. Good. Now press that button on the side of the gearshift and slowly push it forward. Once the boat moves, you can release the button."

Nervously, she followed his instructions and the boat jolted forward with a mighty roar. Panicking, she pulled the shift back to neutral.

"You're doing fine, Susannah. Try it again, only slower."

She did as he said and the front of the boat rose up but then immediately settled back down at a steady speed.

"You've got it!" Gabriel cheered. "Now, it'll go wherever you steer. Reverse is simply from neutral backwards."

Susannah had no idea driving a boat could be so exhilarating! She tried to hide her pleasure from Gabriel, but the sense of power the boat gave her was intoxicating. "This is fantastic!" she shrieked.

She drove the remaining distance to Pinawa Dam, but argued with Gabriel over which of them would dock it. He insisted she was perfectly capable, since there was no dock. When the dam came into sight, she saw he was right. There was no dock, only a bald protrusion of rock sloping gently into the river.

Susannah cut the engine as Gabriel had instructed, and he jumped into the water to prevent the boat from scraping its bottom on the rock, anchoring it by tying a rope around a huge boulder.

Calvin and Chad jumped into the shallow water and headed towards shore. Susannah peered hesitantly into the river.

Gabriel waded over and before she had time to protest, lifted her out of the boat and into the water. "There aren't any leeches."

The physical contact had her pulse racing. Flustered, she thrust his hands from her waist. "You manipulated me into driving that boat."

"Moi?"

Ineffectually, she stamped a foot, splashing them both with water. "You know what I mean. I either had to prove my undying trust or appear like some chicken in front of my boys. I – I just don't think it was very –" she groped for a word, "nice."

He placed his hands on his hips and chuckled. "I confess. I was devious and underhanded."

Susannah stubbornly held her ground. "You most certainly were."

He was still grinning. "Would you like to drive again when we go home?"

She struggled to maintain her frown. Darn him anyway. She couldn't help but giggle. "I most certainly would!" He took her hand and, laughing, they caught up to the boys on shore.

The shoreline demonstrated clearly what the river bed consisted of: enormous expanses of rock. Gabriel led them across terrain which likely had once been the bottom of the river. There was no beach, only large flat rock, and where the ancient river bed ended, a haphazard forest began.

Their ambulations took them alongside miniature swamps and smaller protrusions of rocks until they stood overlooking a crevice at the bottom of which narrow rapids rushed headlong into the river. The opposite bank sat much higher and was crowded with sunbathers.

"That's why I prefer to come by boat," Gabriel said as he indicated the occupants on the other side. "We have to do a bit of climbing, but it's never crowded. The only trouble is, in order to slide down the rapids, we have to cross down there." He pointed to a short span of waterfall which marked the end of the rapids.

"Can't we simply swim at the bottom of the falls?" Susannah asked in alarm. Gabriel hadn't described Pinawa Dam. She had expected water pouring over a dam, a beach and a place to swim.

There was a dam, situated on the horizon, and it was obvious it hadn't been used in decades. It reminded her of the ruins of some ancient civilization.

"We'll walk over to the dam later," Gabriel said. "It's overgrown with weeds in many places, but there are remains of a foot bridge across the top parts of it."

He grimaced at the overpopulated bank facing them. "We spent many hours here as kids, but it was relatively unknown then. Now it's a Heritage Park, with hot dog carts, campgrounds and admission fees ... unless you arrive by boat."

Chad tugged at the hem of Gabriel's cutoffs and pointed to the swimmers in the rapids. "Do we get to swim down the waterfall?"

Susannah drew in a sharp breath, but Gabriel touched her arm reassuringly. "If they wear life jackets, they'll be fine."

She eyed the water. "I don't think I want to cross that waterfall."

"I'll help you over. The current's a bit strong, but you won't hurt yourself even if you do fall. There's a pool of water at the bottom."

She debated, knowing he was waiting patiently for her trust. She brought her eyes up to his and gave him a weak smile. "Who goes first?"

A nearly imperceptible flash of relief passed over his face as he accepted Calvin's enthusiastic "I will! I will!"

Calvin negotiated the crossing amidst fits of giggles with Gabriel firmly clasping his arm as the force of the water lifted him off his feet and threatened to sweep him away.

Chad's crossing was less than smooth. He wailed loudly and had to be carried.

"Would you like to be carried too?" Gabriel asked with outstretched arms when he returned for Susannah.

"Hah! Wouldn't you be surprised if I don't need help?"

He took her arm, laughing softly. "Actually, no, I wouldn't be."

The force of the water nearly pushed Susannah over as it rushed against her legs. She clung to Gabriel out of need rather than fear.

Once they were all safely on the other side of the river, he led them to the top of the rapids and suggested he go first so he could be at the bottom to catch the boys.

Susannah watched him slip into the water and be carried away. She waited a moment or two before sending first Calvin and then Chad. Anxiety gnawed at her as their little bodies floated around a boulder and out of sight.

"Gabriel said he would catch them," she said aloud, as if voicing the words would make them true. She fought the compulsion to run back to the falls to verify her sons' safety. "They'll be okay," she coaxed herself. "Gabriel's there." Suddenly, it occurred to her that it was true. Gabriel would be there, because he had said so. She really could trust him. And more than that, she realized that she did. Beyond a doubt.

Without even thinking about what she was doing, she slipped into the water, sat down and was immediately propelled down the rapids. It was like being on a crude water slide. She was twisted and tossed and pulled under the water and thrown out of it again. She would have been having fun, but her mind was nowhere near the rapids she was in. It was with Gabriel Desjarlais.

She knew he would be faithful to his promise. He would be in her life for as long as she wanted him to be. The knowledge stunned her.

She continued to bounce limply through the rapids until a hand grabbed her arm, pulling her to her feet.

"You were headed for the falls," Gabriel exclaimed. "How was ..."

Susannah stared at him in silence. Droplets of water ran unheeded off her hair and into her eyes which remained fixed upon him.

He wiped a strand of hair from her cheek. "Are you alright?"

She continued to stare, making no sound. What did it all mean? Did he love her? Why had he pushed himself into their lives until they were incomplete without him? Why did her heart thrill at the certainty of his presence? Did she love him? The thought was shocking. But, of course, untrue. She couldn't possibly love Gabriel, could she? She shook her head as if to shake the thoughts away and heard Gabriel ask her if she had a headache.

He led her to the dry, rocky shore, made her sit down and passed her one of the tins of cola they had brought along.

"Here, drink this. Maybe you've had too much sun."

"Yes, I'm sure that's it," she answered weakly, hoping he couldn't somehow guess her thoughts.

"Put on my cap and rest in the shade for a few minutes. I'll take the boys for a tour of the dam."

Susannah nodded her consent and pretended to relax in the shade. Gabriel called out to Calvin and Chad who were occupied with the frogs in a nearby puddle of water. He cast a frown her way before heading off with the boys.

When they were out of sight, she sat up and put her head in her hands. What was she going to do? Did she want Gabriel in her life? Her head told her no, but her heart pounded a definitive yes. Did that mean she loved him? She thought he was one of the most considerate and caring men she had ever met, and definitely handsome, but did that constitute love?

It's infatuation, she told herself, realizing it was the only logical explanation. A schoolgirl crush. The thought had her giggling. A big crush albeit, but she could live with it. Crushes passed, and so would this one, preferably long before Gabriel found the wife he was purportedly in search of. In the meantime, she would allow him to be part of their lives for as long as he wanted. If she solicitously impressed upon Calvin and Chad the impermanence of Gabriel, they would accept his departure more readily when the time came.

Susannah sighed with relief. It was incredibly freeing to have Gabriel sorted out in her mind. Now she could simply enjoy his company, and she was anxious to do just that.

She straightened up, extracted a brush from her

cotton beach bag and pulled it through her damp hair. Scanning the horizon, she spotted Gabriel and the boys waving to her from the top of the dam. She waved back, wondering with a smile who was having more fun, Gabriel or the boys.

When he returned with the boys, Susannah was waiting, refreshed and content.

"Was it ever cool!" Calvin babbled as he plunked himself onto the blanket beside her.

His brother followed suit. "Yeah! An' we saw tunnels and stuff and places for ninjas to hide."

"Except," interjected Calvin gravely, with great sympathy for Gabriel, "they didn't have ninjas when Gabriel was a kid."

"You're looking better." Gabriel smiled as he joined them on the blanket.

She gave him her best smile. "I'm feeling better thanks. I'll have to be sure to bring a hat next time I'm going to be out in the sun so long."

They spent the remainder of the afternoon sliding down the rapids, lazing in the sun and nibbling the lunch Susannah had brought. The boys eventually tired of the rapids and wandered off to chase frogs.

"There's a wedding social next weekend for a cousin of mine," Gabriel said as he put the cap back on a bottle of sunscreen. "I was hoping you would come with me."

Susannah eyed him warily and bit a lip. "Do you mean like come along ... or ... as your date?"

He lay down on his back and placed his cap over his face as if to screen it from the sun, but it didn't fully conceal his amusement. "As my date ... definitely as my date."

She turned her face to hide her delight in case he could still see through his cap. She modulated her voice to nonchalance. "Sure, that would be okay."

"My family's going to be there," he said from under his hat.

She whipped her head around. "Your family?"

"Sure."

"Your whole family?"

"Yes, as in my mother, sisters and other sundry relatives."

"Can I change my mind?"

He lifted the cap from his face to grin at her. "Would you prefer my mother cook dinner and you can meet them all at my house?"

"Dinner at your house?"

What had begun as the jitters about meeting his family was now escalating to total panic.

"I'd like you to meet my family, Susannah." His voice was solemn. "I thought you would be more comfortable in public than at my home."

She stared at him, eyes wide with terror. Going out in public with him would be tribulation enough without the added pressure of meeting his family. They would be comparing her to his previous women, not that she necessarily counted herself as his current woman. Nevertheless, she couldn't bear to be under their scrutiny.

"They're wonderful people, Susannah, and I know they'll love you."

She gulped down the rising hysteria.

His eyes pleaded. "You'd be doing it for me. I'm asking you to come, for me."

She lowered her eyes from the intensity of his gaze. He had never before asked anything of her. She owed it to him to at least consider his request.

In truth, she couldn't imagine his family being anything other than replicas of himself. As for his mother, any woman who had raised such a fine son would have to be very special indeed. She refused to ask herself why it was that Gabriel wanted her to meet his family and instead wondered if meeting them would be as difficult as she feared.

She formed her lips into a smile which she tried to bring to her eyes. "I'd love to meet your family, Gabriel."

Ten

Susannah studied herself in the mirror. Maybe the denim skirt was too casual. She removed it and retrieved the cream, suede skirt from the bed. Holding it up against herself, she reviewed it in the mirror. If she wore the matching vest without a blouse she could remain cool if the hall became hot. It would be less casual than the denim outfit, but was it too sensual without a blouse?

Throwing the skirt on the bed in frustration, she picked up a silk print dress. This was a country social. She could hardly see the women wearing silk dresses. But what if they did? It was, after all, also a wedding social.

Groaning, she flopped backwards onto the bed. She did not want to attract attention to herself by being inappropriately dressed. Being with Gabriel would put her in the spotlight as it was. She couldn't help but smile at the thought and wondered what his wedding social would be like. She laughed as she remembered her and Steven's. It had been almost as fun as the wedding itself, and they'd made enough money off the drink sales to pay for their honeymoon. She imagined Gabriel, as successful as he was, would make enough money to pay for his entire wedding.

"Yoo hoo!" Ada's cheery voice called out from the living room. She had eagerly agreed to baby-sit while Susannah went out with Gabriel.

Susannah sprang from the bed. "I'm nearly finished dressing," she called back, panicking that she still had no idea what to wear. Hastily, she donned the suede outfit. The hem of the vest was fringed, lending itself easily to being worn without a blouse. It made for a lower cut than she was used to wearing, but, she raised an eyebrow with a wily smile, it wouldn't hurt Gabriel to have to suffer through a bit of cleavage!

Her hair had already been arranged into a French twist, but she paused to tug loose a few auburn tendrils. After touching up her lipstick and misting herself with her favourite perfume, she stepped into a pair of cream-coloured pumps and surveyed her appearance.

Her grey eyes darkened with the contrast of the cream outfit and her summer tan. The skirt fit snugly against her curves, and the pumps enhanced her already well-formed legs. She smiled with satisfaction. Who knows? Gabriel Desjarlais might decide he was more than a little interested in her after all.

A low whistle greeted her upon opening the bedroom door. Gabriel stood in the living room with his hands in his pockets. She blushed slightly, but smiled with delight at the appreciation in his eyes. "You are absolutely beautiful."

"Thank you," she said with a shy smile.

"She is indeed," Ada exclaimed. "Now, you folks go on out and have fun. I'll take care of these here boys. We'll play some cards later, but first we're gonna make popcorn balls. Old Bert says he'll come over later."

"All right!" Calvin and Chad whooped as they "high-fived" one another.

Ada shook her hands at Susannah and Gabriel. "Go on and git. The boys'll be just fine."

She nudged Gabriel and gave him a wink as she pushed them out the door. "And if you don't wanna bring her home right after the social, that's okay cause I'll probably be asleep on the couch."

Gabriel laughed and winked at Susannah. "Now, Ada, what would there be for us to do after the social was over?"

The old woman cackled. "I'm sure you'll think of something."

Outside, Susannah was surprised when Gabriel led her up to the road rather than the dock.

"You didn't think I'd take a beautiful woman out for a date in my old boat, did you?"

"It's hardly an old boat, and you do use it like a car–" Susannah stopped short. Her eyes fell upon a late model, fire-engine-red Corvette convertible. "Wow!"

He grinned as he opened her door. "That was exactly my thought when you came out of your room looking like you do."

Her response was a deep red flush as she feigned preoccupation with the leather upholstery. Sinking into the seat, she uttered another "Wow" as he opened his door.

He climbed in beside her, his pleasure obvious in his eyes. "Like I said ... beautiful."

Unused to his compliments, she replied shyly, "You don't look so bad yourself."

Her compliment was a decided understatement. He was wearing black dress pants and a white, cotton dress shirt, neither of which could harness his raw masculinity. Nor had a comb been able to tame the dark waves that hung idly about his collar.

His eyes, dark as night, consumed her. He stared for a moment and then lowered his eyes to her hand, briefly, before raising them again, his gaze penetrating. He placed an arm on the back of Susannah's seat. "Susannah, I'm not in the habit of dating another man's woman."

Her eyes opened wide with startled confusion.

He clasped her hand and fingered Steven's rings. "Tonight, I want you to be my woman."

She chewed her lower lip, understanding fully.

His tone was sad. "If I could spare you this, I would."

She snatched her hand from him and faced the window, leaning on an arm, tears threatening at the corners of her eyes.

Through her tears she searched the cloudy heavens above. What would Steven want? He probably wouldn't even like Gabriel had they ever met. Their lifestyles were completely different. Neither would have been able to comprehend the other.

However, Steven had always placed the welfare of Susannah and their sons above everything. He would not have wanted her to pine her life away. He would have approved of the way Gabriel took an interest in Calvin and Chad.

She stole a glance at Gabriel. He was staring out his window, his head resting against the frame, one arm on the steering wheel. She noticed how vulnerable he suddenly seemed, as if for once he were unsure of himself.

Her heart melted. He hadn't asked for a lifetime commitment. He was merely asking that she come as his date for the evening and not as Steven's widow. He was asking her to let go of the past and to live in the present.

Wiping the tears, Susannah stared down at her wedding rings. Gabriel was right. It was time to take them off. Giving them a tug and a twist, she pulled them from her finger and placed them in her purse. Pulling out a Kleenex, she dabbed at her eyes.

She turned to Gabriel. He had been watching her. They stared at one another in silence. He shifted towards her, his eyes never leaving hers as he gathered her in his arms and stared down at her, murmuring her name. Susannah shivered as his mouth covered hers; she'd never known a kiss more tender. Her hand fluttered to his cheek. He pressed a kiss into it, then clasped it with his own, and crushed her against the seat as his kisses exploded with fierce and unrestrained fury, devouring her. Susannah was drunk with the taste of him, drowning in his wine as he ravaged her cheeks, her eyes, her throat ... he stopped and breathed against her before dragging himself away. He raked his hands through his hair, inhaling several deep breaths. "If we don't drive away right now, we may never go anywhere."

Delicious waves were pulsating through her as she lay back against the seat. She smiled dreamily. "Are we in some sort of rush?"

"Definitely," he grinned, his dark eyes glittering devilishly as he turned the key in the ignition, "because being a gentleman is new for me and damned hard!"

Susannah blushed deeply but couldn't help giggling as the car roared into motion. She cast an eye out the window and caught her reflection in the side-view mirror, noting that what little makeup she wore was now smudged with tears, and her lips were swollen from Gabriel's kisses.

Searching her purse, she found her makeup and commenced repairing her face. Gabriel watched her ministrations with a sideways glance. "It's far more interesting watching you put on makeup than it was my sisters. It seemed like I was always last in line for the shower," he quipped as he steered the car off the gravel road and onto paved highway.

There was something intimate about his watching her apply her makeup, and to avoid blushing, Susannah turned to survey the passing countryside. The terrain, being further from the river, had transitioned from trees and rocks to fields and farmhouses, offset by a horizon which stretched out endlessly beyond.

"The immense flatness of the prairies has always awed me," she said at last, breaking the silence. "The sky seems to start right at the ground."

Gabriel grinned. "I see my kisses bring out the poet in you."

This time Susannah knew he could see the heat of her blush. Gabriel slowed the car. "They also seem to have made you extraordinarily shy. Maybe I should pull over and help you become more familiar with me."

Susannah laughed. But he brought the car to a halt and reached over. He imprisoned her in his arms and said huskily, "You thought I was joking, didn't you?" He traced a finger over her lips. Susannah nodded breathlessly. "Shall I kiss you?" He didn't wait for permission as his lips met hers.

"BEEP" a horn blared loudly behind them.

They sprang apart in surprise.

"Hey, Gabriel, I thought maybe that old antique of yours had broke down or something," a heavy-set man yelled from behind the wheel of a pickup truck. His bearded face broke into a leering grin. "But I can see that ain't the kind of trouble you're in."

Gabriel laughed as the pickup rolled back onto the

highway, its occupants waving a grinning goodbye. "That was my sister, Mary, and her husband."

Susannah slid down her seat, thoroughly mortified at having been caught kissing in a car like a pair of teenagers. "I think I want to go home," she said with a sickly smile and groan.

Gabriel's eyes sparkled. "I could tell you a few stories about Greg and Mary before they got married, including the time I discovered them in the hay loft."

"Yes, well that's fine if you're an adolescent."

He flashed a smile as he put the car into gear. "You're never too old for love, Susannah."

A short time later, they pulled into the gravelled parking lot of a quaint old church whose wooden siding boasted a fresh coat of white paint.

"What a charming little church!" Susannah exclaimed as she stepped out of the car.

Gabriel came round to her and linked his arm in hers. "My folks were married here. I was christened here. My sisters were married here, and my father is buried out back."

He escorted her to a side door from which the bouncing strains of a polka could be heard. They walked down a set of stairs leading into a basement hall.

At the bottom of the steps a petite young woman dressed in a black spandex minidress greeted them. "Hey, Gabriel! How's it going?"

"This is my niece, Solange Chartrand," Gabriel told Susannah as the girl took his tickets and stamped their hands with blue ink.

Solange flicked her long black hair from her face and smiled at Susannah. "And you must be Susannah. Everyone's been talking about how Uncle Gabriel was bringing his woman tonight. I hope you're ready to be attacked by a bunch of old biddies."

"Take it easy, Solange," Gabriel laughed. "Susannah might turn and run."

Keeping his arm to the small of her back, he guided her into the hall. It was fairly dark, but she could easily see long tables lined up along the sides of the hall and crowds of people noisily enjoying themselves. The dance floor consisted of the tiled expanse between the two rows of tables and was occupied with folks dancing a rousing polka.

A blonde woman noticed them standing in the entrance and motioned to her partner. The couple ceased dancing and made their way towards Susannah and Gabriel.

"Well hello!" The woman greeted them with a broad smile before giving Gabriel a kiss on the cheek.

"This is my sister, Zofia, and her husband, Jean-Marc. Solange is their daughter," Gabriel said as the woman reached for Susannah's hand.

"We've been dying to meet you, Susannah, ever since Gabriel started whistling that silly song. Our baby sister, Ghislaine, says she's going to fax us the words from Winnipeg once she finds a copy of them, so that we can all tease him by singing it."

Susannah smiled back at Zofia. So, teasing was a family trait after all. Zofia was a very attractive woman. Her fair skin and hair were a sharp contrast to Gabriel's dark features, but she still possessed the same deep brown eyes.

Zofia glanced at Gabriel. "Mom is probably in the kitchen, as usual, and Mary is here somewhere."

Gabriel slid Susannah a sly grin. "Yes, they passed us on the road."

"How old is Zofia?" Susannah asked as Gabriel directed her towards the kitchen.

"Thirty-three"

"She must have had Solange while still a baby herself."

Gabriel grinned. "Sometimes we get an early start in the country, but I notice you appear to have been in a bit of a rush yourself."

"How old are you?"

"Thirty-six."

"Why are you so slow?"

His eyes twinkled merrily. "I've been waiting for the right woman."

Susannah couldn't help but wonder who that woman would be.

Their advance towards the kitchen was impeded by people approaching Gabriel for an introduction to Susannah. Most of them were relatives of one sort or another, ranging from aunts and uncles to thrice-removed cousins, although a few were former school mates or neighbours. Many of them spoke French as well as English, and some spoke Polish. Gabriel replied in English, taking care not to exclude Susannah unless, of course, the speaker spoke no English whatsoever, in which case Gabriel translated.

A few times Susannah was invited to dance, but Gabriel hastily declined on her behalf, subduing even the most persistent of suitors with a black scowl. She had to hide her smile whenever he fended off even the slightest attention from another man. One gentleman had gone so far as to gallantly offer to fetch Susannah a drink, but Gabriel dealt with him in a similar fashion. After watching the intruder beat a hasty retreat, Gabriel turned to her. "I've been remiss. Would you like something to drink?"

Biting back a chortle, Susannah choked out, "Yes, please. I'd like a cola."

"You don't drink?"

"Not much, a glass or two of wine sometimes."

She watched him leave to fetch the cola and giggled. His possessiveness pleased her. She was smugly reminding herself what Zofia had said about him whistling "Oh Susannah" when a woman sidled up to her.

"So this is Gabriel's little Susannah."

The hair stood up on the back of Susannah's neck. She turned to see a tall, buxom blonde dressed in a red version of Solange's tight little dress. Unfortunately, what looked cute on Solange, looked silly on this older woman.

Putting on her most professional face, Susannah extended her hand. "If you mean is my name Susannah and am I here with Gabriel Desjarlais, then yes."

The woman grasped Susannah's hand limply. "We've all been wondering what Gabriel's latest little toy looked like. I must say, you are cute, aren't you?"

Gabriel arrived with the drinks, sparing Susannah the trouble of a response. "I see you've met Dawn Kaminski. She's Greg's sister and therefore family of sorts."

Dawn's ruby red lips pouted at Gabriel while her hand crawled up his arm. "Surely, Gabriel, you could find a more intimate definition of our relationship than that."

Careful not to spill his drink, he disengaged his arm. "We'll have to catch you later, Dawn; we were on our way to the kitchen to introduce Susannah to my mother."

Dawn pouted. "Well make sure you do catch me later ... I'll be waiting."

When they were out of Dawn's earshot, Susannah

batted her eyelashes at Gabriel, mimicking Dawn's sultry voice, "Surely, you can find a more intimate definition of our relationship?"

He let out a loud guffaw. "Why, Susannah James, I believe you're jealous."

She snorted. "Of that woman? Ha!"

He took a sip of his drink, and she peeped into his glass. "What are you drinking?"

"Cola."

"You don't drink either?"

"Sometimes. It's not something I make a habit of."

Susannah was relieved. She had never felt the need or desire to get drunk in order to have fun or relax around others. She and Steven had shared an occasional bottle of wine and the odd social drink, but for the most part, they had abstained.

Arriving at the door to the kitchen, they peeked inside to see several older women busily arranging food on trays. A slim, silver-haired woman looked up.

"Gabriel!" she exclaimed as she left her post to embrace him. She turned to grasp Susannah's cheeks in her soft hands. "So this is Gabriel's Susannah." Mrs. Desjarlais glanced back at her son while taking Susannah's hand. "She is even more beautiful than you described. And look now how I've made her blush."

She called out in Polish to the women and then switched to French. The women swarmed Susannah en masse with a chorus of "ah's." They milled about her while Gabriel's mother introduced them one by one, many of them relations.

Susannah did not try to commit anyone's name to memory, but rather nodded and offered a "Pleased to meet you" with each introduction, all the while making a study of Mrs. Desjarlais.

She spoke with only the slightest Polish accent, which lent well to her graceful carriage and awarded her an aura of elegance. She was quite attractive for her age, and Susannah thought she must have been very beautiful in her youth.

Upon Mrs. Desjarlais' announcement that Ada Semchuk had been teaching Susannah to cook, the women dragged Susannah over to various trays of food and commenced to brag over what each of them had made while offering to teach how to prepare it.

To her relief, Gabriel intervened, pulling her by the arm and saying loudly as he pushed her out of the kitchen, "Oh no you don't. She's coming out for a dance with me."

Susannah giggled. "Thank you. I thought I was going to end up buried under all that food."

His eyes surveyed the dance floor. "Ah yes, but there is a price for my gallantry." His eyes wandered back to hers. "You owe me a dance."

It was Susannah's turn to scan the dance floor. Rock and roll music had been playing while they were in the kitchen, but now a polka dictated the dance steps. "I've never danced a polka."

"Really? You've been to a social before, haven't you?"

"Yes, but Steven didn't enjoy dancing."

"Can you waltz? I mean a real waltz, not that thing teenagers do."

"Yes."

He drew her arms into a dance pose. "Well, it's sort of like a waltz, but faster, and you hop, but not really."

She giggled. "Well that really clarified it for me."

He laughed and led her to the middle of the dance floor. She tried to follow his instructions but succeeded only in giving his feet a few good stomps.

"It's a good thing you're not fat, or I'd have no feet left," he teased.

Susannah moaned. "Maybe we should give up. I'll never get the hang of this."

He gave her a slow grin. "Don't try so hard. I don't believe there's anything you can't learn to do."

Challenged, Susannah persisted, while both of them laughed at her efforts, but eventually she was dancing a polka as well as anyone else.

"That certainly was a workout," she panted when the music finally stopped.

Keeping her hand in his, he led her to a table. Before reaching it, a woman blocked their path.

"Hello, Gabriel." An attractive brunette smiled at him.

Gabriel looked uncomfortable. "Susannah, this is Lisa Penner. She's a teacher at the local school."

Lisa smiled politely at Susannah. "I hear you have two sons. Maybe I will end up with one of them in my class."

They exchanged small talk regarding Calvin and Chad for a few moments, but Susannah noticed Lisa looked only at Gabriel when she spoke. There had definitely been something between them. A sick feeling churned inside Susannah. Was Lisa Penner the woman he wanted? What if his sole motive for bringing her tonight was to make this woman jealous?

Lisa had been chatting about the school when Gabriel interrupted, side-stepping her. "Please excuse us, Lisa. Susannah has not yet met all of my family, and I can see Mary eagerly waving us over." The woman who had waved at them from the pickup indicated the vacant chairs beside her.

"I guess we've sort of already met," Mary giggled as Susannah sat down.

She was a younger version of Gabriel, having the same dark complexion and wavy hair. The strong lines of his face had been softened on hers, producing a classic beauty.

"You'll be glad to hear you have now more or less met the entire family," Mary chattered. "Ghislaine, has moved to Winnipeg to attend university and Lise is working in Toronto."

Mary's discourse was cut short by the arrival of the engaged couple, in whose honour the social was being held. The disc jockey encouraged a round of applause, and everyone stood up to welcome them.

Susannah thought they were terribly young to be getting married until she reminded herself that she had been a mere eighteen at her own social.

Mary leaned over while clapping. "They're both my cousins. Can you believe it? One from the Polish side and one from the French."

Before everyone had sat back down, Gabriel was called away by Mary's husband to help tend the bar. "I'm sure the family chatterbox will keep you entertained until I return," he laughingly told Susannah as he departed, dodging a playful punch from Mary.

It certainly is a tightly-knit community, Susannah thought as they watched the engaged couple formally commence the evening with a slow, romantic waltz. She could not imagine an outsider like herself ever fitting in.

"So! Somebody actually managed to capture my brother's heart."

Susannah turned to Mary in surprise. "Pardon me?"

"Countless women have tried without success."

"Yes, and I'm beginning to suspect half of them are here in this very room."

Mary laughed, sounding a lot like her brother.

"You could be right." She sipped her drink. "We were beginning to wonder if we were ever going to meet you. He kept putting us off, saying we'd scare you away. Finally we threatened to pile into our trucks and drive over. That's when he said he'd bring you to the social."

Susannah was at a loss for words. Gabriel's family had obviously been well aware of his visits to her cottage.

Mary squeezed Susannah's arm. "I can hardly wait to get to know you better. If my brother fell in love, then you must be very special."

"I'm not so sure I would define Gabriel's feelings toward me as love," Susannah replied hastily.

"Are you blind?" Mary asked. "He's absolutely wild about you. We've never seen him like this before. And when he told us he let you drive the boat! You had to pick me up off the floor! Nobody drives Gabriel's boat!" Warmed to her topic, Mary gushed, "I'm surprised he's left your side long enough to actually tend the bar. Just look at him! He hasn't taken his eyes off you."

Hesitantly, Susannah raised her eyes across the room. She started. Gabriel was looking straight at her. When their eyes met, he winked.

"He's probably worried someone will ask you to dance while he's away," Mary giggled. "I don't think he has anything to worry about though. Rumour has it he scared away anyone who came within ten feet of you."

"I think you're exaggerating a little."

Mary threw back her head to laugh. "Really? Well I'll bet the only person who asks you to dance tonight is Gabriel himself!"

Susannah's stomach was doing little flips. Was Mary right? Was he in love with her? The very possibility made her giddy.

Mary's mischievous grin was a duplicate of Gabriel's. "I'll also bet you're crazy in love with him too."

Blushing, Susannah shifted uncomfortably on her chair. "I haven't fully decided what my feelings towards Gabriel are."

Mary let out a loud guffaw. "Honey, that's something that's decided for you. Whether or not to accept his marriage proposal – well I suppose that's something you'll have to decide." Mary stopped just long enough to sip from her glass. "He told us you used to be a bank manager."

Susannah nodded, relieved the topic had changed.

Mary inclined her head in her brother's direction, her eyes gravely dark. "I hope you can understand that he needs a wife who will be devoted to him and the farm. You wouldn't have time for a career."

Susannah carefully steered the conversation away from Gabriel. "I haven't decided what I want to do, career-wise. Leaving the bank was a last-minute decision. But I'm not sure I want to go back to it. I wouldn't mind trying something completely different." She paused. "Did you never want a career, Mary?"

"I did attend university for about two years. I was planning on becoming a veterinarian."

"Why didn't you?"

"Greg and I were living together. I wanted to study, and he wanted to be with me. He worked as a mechanic while I went to school." Mary paused. "It nearly drove Gabriel crazy that we weren't married, but it was my choice, not his."

Susannah grinned. "I have no difficulty believing that Gabriel is a protective brother."

Mary laughed in agreement. "Anyway, Greg

wasn't cut out for city life. He missed the farm, and when his Dad wanted to retire and give him the business, he had to choose between me and it."

"What happened?"

"He would have given up the farm if I had asked, but I loved him too much to watch him waste away in the city. He would never have been content. It was a tough decision to make, but I gave up my studies and came back here with him."

"Do you have regrets?"

Mary smiled sweetly. "None whatsoever. I discovered I could be fulfilled without a career. I sort of have one anyway. We own a dairy farm. It's long hours and a lot of work. It belongs to both of us. We're a team. It's made for a real bond between us. I love Greg now more than I ever have." She leaned close and whispered, "I better, because we found out today that I'm definitely pregnant."

Susannah's smile was bright and warm, understanding the joy of a first pregnancy. "I'm thrilled for you!"

"Shh! We haven't told anyone yet."

"Why am I so privileged?"

Mary laughed. "Well, for one thing, I'm nearly bursting with the news." She squeezed Susannah's hand. "But it's also my little way of welcoming you into the family."

Susannah frowned. While Mary had been chattering, she had glanced towards the bar and noticed that Gabriel was no longer there. Searching the room, she spotted him a few tables away, entangled in Dawn Kaminski's arms. Dawn appeared to be quite comfortably running her hands over his chest.

Livid, Susannah turned back to Mary who was still chattering. When she finished, Susannah blurted, "I certainly hope you don't end up too disappointed if things don't work out between Gabriel and myself."

A deep voice interrupted their conversation. "Now why wouldn't they?" Gabriel was leaning over behind her, amused. She glared at him. "Susannah, you look as if you'd like to dance," he teased.

"You have no idea what I'd like," she ground out.

He laughed. "May I please have this dance?"

She stood up and permitted him to lead her to the dance floor.

"Are you sure it's me you want?" she demanded snidely as they commenced to waltz. Ignoring his raised eyebrow, she continued hotly. "Is there any woman in this room you haven't slept with?"

He broke into laughter. "You're jealous!"

"I am not! I just happen to think it's a bit of a double standard that I am not allowed to dance with anyone else while you may grope every little sex-kitten which crosses your path."

They had all but stopped dancing. "If you're referring to Dawn Kaminski, perhaps those jealous eyes of yours should have watched a little longer. You would have seen me push her away. And, I never said you couldn't dance with another man."

Susannah stomped a foot. "No, of course you didn't. You didn't have to. You made sure no one would be foolish enough to risk your wrath by doing so."

His eyes twinkled with mischief. "Is there someone in particular with whom you'd like to dance?"

"That's not the point."

"Is there?"

"That's not the point."

"Admit it. You're jealous."

"I am not."

He let go of her hands, stood back and stretched

out his arms in a gesture of surrender. "I confess. I would like to clobber any man who so much as looks in your direction. Now it's your turn. Admit you're jealous."

Stunned by his confession, Susannah looked around her and realized other couples were eyeing her and Gabriel with interest.

He moved closer and murmured in her ear as he drew her into a dance again. "Admit that you're jealous or I'm going to give you such a passionate kiss, right here on the dance floor, that when you come up for air, you won't remember your name, let alone all the people watching."

Her feet barley moving, she lifted her head. Jealous? His eyes drew her in, drowning her in them. No, she wasn't jealous. She was in love. She knew it now. This was no schoolgirl crush. She knew at last what she suspected Gabriel had known all along. She had been in love with him from the moment they met.

Unable to speak, she could only mouth a "Yes," her grey eyes large and round with the depth of her emotion.

Clutching her tightly, Gabriel whispered, "I still want to give you that kiss." He moved his mouth over hers.

Disquieted by the certainty of an audience, Susannah struggled to maintain her equilibrium. But as his kiss deepened in intensity, her world began to spin, and she surrendered completely, until all she was aware of was him and her love.

He drew his mouth from hers, leaving her limp and leaning against him and gasping for breath. They continued in a languid dance. "Let's leave," he murmured against her neck.

Hypnotically, she inclined her head in acquiescence. He wrapped his arm around her waist and escorted her from the dance floor.

"You aren't leaving already?" Zofia called out as Gabriel scooped Susannah's purse from the table.

He stopped in front of Zofia and Jean-Marc. "I've done my duty. You've all met her. I'm claiming the remainder of the evening for myself."

Zofia laughed. "I suppose I can't argue with that." Pausing to press Susannah's hand in her own, she added softly, "It's been a joy to meet you at last. Perhaps Gabriel will bring you for a real visit with the family soon, and we will have more time to get to know you better."

"Okay, that's it! Time's up," Gabriel announced impatiently as he wrenched her hand from his sister's grasp, leaving Susannah time for only a brief wave to Mary who giggled as she waved back.

He kept his arm around her waist as they crossed the parking lot to his car. Before opening her door, he gave her a light kiss. "Let's go back and get rid of Ada."

She gave him a wry smile. "I suppose next you'll tell me all we'll do is talk."

He stepped back and bowed, grinning devilishly. "I surrender my will to the lady. We will do whatever you wish."

Susannah opened the car door and seated herself inside, laughing as she rolled down the window. "Great! I wish you to be the one to get rid of Ada."

He leaned his head inside and kissed her. "No problem. I've been dealing with Ada all my life."

She relaxed against the leather as he climbed in and started up the motor. "Why did you mislead me into thinking you didn't want me?"

His utter surprise was written all over his face. "Is that what you thought?"

She nodded.

"Because I tried so hard not to kiss you before tonight?"

She nodded again.

"Susannah, the only thing that kept me away from you was your rings."

He pulled the car over to the shoulder. Lifting her hand to his mouth, he kissed the finger so recently vacated of its rings. "I figured you would be ready for me when you decided you didn't need them anymore."

The touch of his lips made her skin tingle. "But you ended up having to ask me to remove them."

His smile was tender. "I couldn't take you to meet my family with another man's rings on your hand. I had to gamble on you're coming with me as meaning you were ready to take them off."

"What if I hadn't been?"

He sighed. "Then I guess I would have had to continue developing my newly acquired patience." He grinned. "I didn't want to pressure you, but keeping my distance has just about killed me."

"Really?"

Gabriel put the car into gear and pulled onto the highway. He slid her a crooked grin. "Really."

Susannah looked up at the stars and smiled. Apparently her powers of perception were not as finely tuned as she had believed.

Eleven

Except for the back porch light, the cottage was dark when Gabriel's Corvette pulled onto the parkway at the rise of the hill. "Ada must be asleep," he said, turning off the engine.

Hand in hand, they strolled down the darkened path to the cottage. Susannah looked up at the night sky peeping through the trees and recalled her first confused amble down the path. How different her life had been then. Who could have foretold she would be walking down this very same path, in love with the man who now held her hand?

She snuck a sideways glance at Gabriel. Yes, she did love him but ... would he now expect her to sleep with him? She couldn't blame him if he did, given the way she had thrown herself at him the other night.

The real question was should she sleep with him? She wanted to, but he hadn't said anything about love. She wasn't sure she could give herself to him without that. She wasn't sure she could, even if he did tell her he loved her. When she had made love with Steven for the first time, she had been his wife. Would a confession of love be enough security for her to abandon herself to Gabriel?

Knowing Ada waited in the cottage gave her

comfort. Maybe she could insist Ada stay for tea. She nearly giggled when she pictured Gabriel's frustration over Ada's prolonged presence.

Soundlessly, he opened the cottage door. Susannah tiptoed inside. Turning on the stove light, she glanced around the cottage. Ada was nowhere in sight. Removing her pumps, she glided towards her sons' rooms and peeked inside. Both were empty.

Anxious, she looked back to Gabriel who had found a note on the table. He read it aloud as she returned to the kitchen. "Boys wanted a sleep-over at our house. Will bring them back in the morning."

"What a conniving old woman!" Susannah sputtered, nervous and making every effort to conceal it. "I can well imagine who put that idea into their heads."

Gabriel chuckled softly but said nothing. They stood staring at each other. He put his arms around her waist and hummed a tune, drawing her into a slow dance. They drifted around the room, so close together they melded as one.

Aware only of an intense yearning mingled with fear, Susannah could not recall when they had ceased to dance and begun to kiss. She imagined Gabriel loving her, and she shivered with anticipation. That he wanted her, she had no doubt. Where did they go from here? She had to decide now before her body made the choice for her.

Sensing her uncertainty, he held her away from him. "Let's sit down and talk this out."

"Gabriel, I'm just not sure if I can ..." she began as she sat down with him on the sofa. "I mean, I want to ... I just don't know if ..."

His eyes were warm as he traced a finger over her face. "I know it wouldn't take much persuasion to get you into the bedroom." He paused. "I won't take advantage of that, Susannah."

She waited for him to continue. "I want our union to be free ... for both of us. I want you to be absolutely certain of what you want. I've never cared about that before."

She opened her mouth, but he hushed her with a hand pressed gently to her lips. "There's something else." He expelled a long sigh. "If I could, I would trade every memory I have of every other woman in exchange for your love." His eyes stared at her intently. "I love you, Susannah. My love is the one thing I have given no other woman."

His words brought tears to her eyes. He touched one with a finger as it fell from her lash. "I can wait until you're ready."

She stared at him through her tears and wondered why her lips refused to form the words she knew he wanted to hear. What kept her from confessing her love? Steven? Her sons?

Those were questions to ponder. She knew the answers would be slow in coming. "You'll wait?"

His smile was tender. "I'll wait."

Hours later, Susannah was making coffee while Gabriel sat at the kitchen table, talking. They had been talking all night, about anything and everything. Every so often they had stopped to kiss. Susannah had changed into sweats and Gabriel had removed his tie. Gabriel was now amusing her with funny little anecdotes about his family.

"You are a bad influence, Gabriel Desjarlais!" Susannah exclaimed as she looked out her kitchen window. "The sun's beginning to rise, and my reputation will be in tatters if Ada catches us."

He laughed and stood up, yawning as he stretched. "You are known by the company you keep," he quipped and stooped down to kiss her. "I must say it's a new experience for me to still need a cold shower after having spent the night with a woman."

Susannah blushed delicately as she laughed.

A high-pitched screech pierced the early morning air, shattering their solitude. "HELP! HELP!"

Gabriel rushed to the back door and was nearly bowled over by Ada Semchuk who burst through screaming at the top of her loud lungs. "Thank God you're still here, Gabriel! It's my Bert. I think he's having a heart attack!"

Gabriel tore off across the yard, while Susannah grabbed Ada's hand, jogging alongside her as she waddled back to her cottage.

They arrived to witness Gabriel already performing CPR on Bert who lay prostrate on the living room floor. Ada stood by helplessly, sobbing uncontrollably.

"Call an ambulance!" Gabriel ordered in between thrusts to Bert's chest.

Susannah raced to the phone, and dialed the volunteer ambulance service with shaking fingers. "This is site 204 on Lee River Road. Bert Semchuk is unconscious with no pulse. CPR is being administered." She spoke anxiously, trying hard to recall her first aid training the bank had insisted all its managers take. "Yes, we'll keep the line clear," she confirmed as she hung up the receiver and then crossed to Ada, catching sight of Calvin and Chad who stood motionless as they watched Gabriel work on Bert.

"Ada, sit down. Gabriel and I will take care of Bert until the ambulance arrives." Susannah brought Calvin and Chad over. "Come sit with Auntie Ada and hold her hand," she urged gently, pausing to brush their tousled hair from their eyes. "You need to be real big grown-up boys and take care of Ada while I help Gabriel."

Ada gratefully accepted the boys gentle comfort as they wrapped their arms around her neck and knelt on the sofa beside her. "Oh Bert! Oh Bert!" she sobbed.

"You must be getting tired," Susannah said as she knelt down beside Gabriel. "Let me take over for a while."

He raised his eyes, the worry in them vivid. She was surprised at how calm she felt. "C'mon, take a break," she urged with a gentle pat.

He nodded and moved aside. Susannah bent over Bert, first giving him the prerequisite breath of air and checking for a pulse. Finding none, she twisted her left hand through her fingers and pulled backwards to expose the ball of her wrist. Locating the correct place on Bert's chest, she commenced the life saving thrusts.

"One, and two, and three, and ..." She counted to fifteen and stopped to evaluate Bert's pulse and breathing. "One, and two, and ..."

When she tired, Gabriel relieved her. They alternated until the ambulance siren could be heard.

"Oh thank heavens!" Ada exclaimed as she pulled herself off the sofa and hurried to the door.

Two ambulance attendants rushed into the cottage with a stretcher and an assortment of equipment. One did an assessment of Bert while the other prepared an oxygen mask and relieved Gabriel. Susannah anxiously eyed the defibrillator lying in wait on the floor. She prayed they would not have to use it.

"We've got a pulse!" yelled the attendant who had been performing CPR. He inserted an oxygen tube into Bert's mouth, after which his partner assisted in moving him to the waiting stretcher.

Ada followed the stretcher to the ambulance, and

the attendants assisted her climb inside before closing the door and driving away, the siren screaming ahead of them.

Susannah stared after the flashing lights of the ambulance. When she turned back, Calvin and Chad were crying in the cottage doorway.

"Is Bert dead?" Calvin asked.

Gabriel gathered him up into his arms. "No way, buddy! Old Bert is not going to die."

Susannah wrenched Calvin from him. "How can you be so sure?" she demanded viciously.

Gabriel looked shocked at first, then his face softened. "It's been a terrible experience for all of us," he said softly. "Come, let's put the boys back to bed."

Susannah followed him along the path to her cottage. He was carrying both boys. Her heart beat wildly. Right before their eyes, her sons had watched a man nearly die. A man she was sure they loved.

Gabriel was ushering Calvin and Chad to their rooms when Susannah entered the cottage. "They can sleep together," she said tightly.

He made no reply, but permitted Chad to pass into Calvin's room. He made as if to follow him in, but Susannah intercepted him, barring the doorway with her body.

"I'll put them down," she stated flatly.

The boys crawled into bed beside one another and rubbed their tired eyes. She murmured over them as she pulled up the covers and tucked them in. "You close your eyes and don't worry. Mommy will find out how Bert is doing later today. In the meantime, think happy thoughts."

She gazed back at them before closing the door. They were already close to sleep, now that they were safe in their own home and cuddled together.

Gabriel waited in the living room, his back to her and his hands in his pockets, deep in thought as he gazed out the window at the approaching dawn.

Hearing her, he turned and gathered her in his arms. "You were very brave, Susannah. Bert might not have made it if it hadn't been for you."

Her mind was drowning in a flood of thoughts. She tore herself from him and putting her hands over her face, sobbed, "I can't do this, Gabriel!"

He ran his hand through his hair in distraction. "I was afraid of this."

She was inexplicably furious with him. "How dare you tell my children that Bert will be okay? How dare you treat them like they mean something to you?"

His expression was pained, but he said nothing and allowed her to vent her rage.

Susannah knew she was being irrational but couldn't help herself. "I don't want you to go near them ever again, and you can stay away from me too, for that matter."

"Sweetheart, you don't know what you're saying right now. Do you think I don't know how hard that was for you?" He took a step toward her. "Don't you think I understand it was like watching Steven die all over again?"

She began to quiver as tears poured from her eyes. He cradled her in his arms, resting her head against his shoulder. She clung to him, desperate for his comfort.

"Hush," he murmured as he stroked and kissed her hair. She lifted her face and found his mouth. He kissed her softly.

He always seemed to know the right things to say. The right things to do. How she loved him! Being with him was right. He was a father to her sons, and they loved him in return. Just like they loved Bert. Just like Bert ...

"No!" she sobbed as she pushed him away. "No! You'll only end up hurting us."

"Susannah, I love you. I would never do anything to hurt you or your sons."

She placed her hands over her ears. "No! Go away!"

"Susannah, how could I hurt you?"

"Because everyone dies sooner or later."

"Of course everyone dies, honey. It's the living in between which counts."

She looked at him through her tears. "I can't risk putting my sons through losing someone they love again. And, I can't put myself through it either."

"Who says you won't die first?"

"I'm cutting down the odds of their having to suffer any more than necessary."

"Don't you think they'll suffer anyway if you send me away?" Gabriel countered.

"They'll get over it."

"And what about you?"

"So will I."

"That's where you're wrong, Susannah. You won't get over it. No one ever does when they run away from life."

She was desperate. If he didn't leave soon he would talk her into letting him stay. "Why are you arguing with me?" she demanded. "You said if I ever wanted you to go away, all I had to do was ask."

"I'm arguing because I love you with my very life."

She held her ground. "You promised."

"Don't do this, Susannah!" The shock on his face revealed his horror. "You know you're twisting my promise. It was intended to be an anchor for you. Not a weapon."

"You said I could trust you. You made a promise."

He paced the room. "Geez, Susannah!" He held his arms tightly at his sides, his fists clenched, as if to prevent himself from grabbing hold of and shaking her.

"You promised," she pressed.

He groaned. "All right. I'll go now, but I'll be back tomorrow."

"I won't change my mind."

He backed towards the door. "Things may look different tomorrow, Susannah."

She remained standing stiffly in the living room, listening to the roar of his car as he angrily spun the tires. As the sound of the car faded into the distance, she fell to the floor, sobbing.

Twelve

He arrived late the following afternoon. She had expected him by boat but the rumbling of a motor vehicle as it stopped at the top of her lot had her thanking the heavens that Calvin and Chad were busy playing on the dock, unaware of Gabriel's arrival. She wiped her hands on a kitchen towel before going out to meet him.

Seeing her, his face lit up, but fell when he caught sight of her countenance. They met halfway up the path and stood facing one another. Arms stiff at her sides, Susannah fought the weakness growing within. All day long she had remained adamant despite the tears which frequently flowed.

Seeing him in the flesh, seeing the pain in his eyes tore her apart. If anything, she loved him more than before. Choking down her weakness, she straightened her shoulders and held his eyes firmly with her own. "Nothing's changed."

His eyes clouded over, but he said nothing and instead turned his back and headed up the hill to his truck, the very pickup which had been the catalyst for their first meeting.

She stared after him, watching him climb back inside. He leaned an arm out the window, staring ahead at the road for a few moments. He turned to her, opened his mouth as if to say something, and then changing his mind, put the truck into gear and drove away.

"Hey! That was Gabriel!" Calvin shouted as he ran up behind Susannah, Chad following at his heels.

Susannah made no response, still staring at the vacant space on the road where his truck had been.

"It was!" Calvin hollered. "Hey, Gabriel! Gabriel!"

"How come he didn't come and see us, Mom?" Chad asked.

She said nothing. The boys ran down the road, chasing after the now-distant tail lights of his truck, calling his name as they went.

She turned to the cabin, slowly making her way down the hill. The boys would be back as soon as his truck rounded the bend, and they could no longer see it. Entering the cottage, she returned to the sink and resumed washing the dishes.

The remainder of the summer passed slowly, dragging itself through the blazing Indian summer which brought in autumn. Susannah dragged along with the days, striving not to sink into the same despair which had marked Steven's death.

Calvin and Chad inquired regularly after Gabriel, but she explained that he had gone away just as she had foretold. They seemed to accept her explanation, although it did nothing to discourage them from keeping a morning vigil on the edge of the dock to watch for him.

She wondered if he noticed them standing forlornly on the dock from across the river. She, herself, avoided the dock like a poison. If they went swimming, she either drove to Pinawa Dam or to the public pool in Lac du Bonnet. Since they had no boat, there was little reason for her to go down to the dock anyway, unless Calvin and Chad required her to look at some new bug or larvae they had found.

One such time, she had been peering over their shoulders at a snapping turtle when she raised her head at the sound of a passing boat. It looked as if it could have been Gabriel's but she couldn't be sure. The boys noticed it too and waved excitedly, calling out his name. The driver had waved in return but from that distance Susannah could not tell if it was him. Her heart beating wildly, she had hastily retreated to the cottage, not daring to look behind her as she had hiked up the hill.

She had contemplated moving back to Winnipeg, but her sons had already undergone too many upheavals to place a new one on the pile. Something else kept her at Lee River. It was Gabriel. The knowledge that he was always somewhere nearby permitted her to feel connected to him in an odd way. Moving would be the final step in casting him from her life.

Some evenings, when she knew it would be too dark for him to see her, she would sit on the edge of the dock after the boys were asleep and stare across the river at the lights and guess which ones were his. She believed she pretty much had it figured out. She would think about him and wonder what he might be doing at that exact moment. Sometimes she would cry and sometimes she wouldn't.

As if sensing her daughter was in trouble, Susannah's mother had begun telephoning at regular intervals. Susannah had considered inviting her down for a visit, but she was afraid of having to answer questions if the boys mentioned Gabriel. Using her grief over the loss of Steven as an excuse, she managed to continue postponing her parents' arrival.

She maintained a cheerful facade in front of her sons. She had abandoned them to her grief once before and was determined never to do so again. However, there were some days when she felt her face would crack from the strain of wearing a smile when all she really wanted to do was lie on her bed and sob.

"Doesn't Gabriel love us anymore?" Chad had inquired sadly one morning at breakfast.

Susannah squeezed his shoulders and sat down at the table beside him. "Of course he does, honey. He always will. He just can't be with us anymore."

"If he loved us he would come back," Calvin had argued moodily as he had joined them at the table.

At such times, Susannah was haunted by guilt. Had she done the right thing? Did he still love them? He probably still loved Calvin and Chad, but he was likely busy drowning his sorrow over Susannah in the warmth of some other woman's arms. She winced at the picture of him embracing Dawn Kaminski. Or perhaps he sought comfort from Lisa Penner. Lisa would no doubt be more than willing to console him.

Bert recovered and came home three weeks after his heart attack. Ada drove him crazy with her cosseting for the first few weeks because he was pretty much confined to the cottage and defenceless against her.

"Gabriel was right. He said you were gonna be okay," the boys had chanted when their beloved Bert had once again sat in his overstuffed armchair.

Calvin and Chad spent endless hours with Bert. He taught them to play checkers and some new card games while Ada merrily baked cookies in her kitchen. Susannah often sought the Semchuks' company as well, sitting herself despondently at Ada's table while the older woman busied herself at the stove.

If Ada suspected the reason for Gabriel's noticeable absence, she never said, other than to quietly whisper when the boys could not hear that he had been by to visit Bert. How Gabriel knew when to come without bumping into Susannah or the boys was a mystery to her. Ada never disclosed his secret, and Susannah never asked.

The absence of Ada's characteristic nosiness set Susannah on edge. She waited for the woman to bring up the subject, but day after day, Ada remained steadfastly silent on that particular topic.

The first day of school arrived to everyone's fear and trepidation. Calvin and Chad were anxious over having to make new friends and meet new teachers. Susannah worried not only over how well they would adjust, but also over what she would do to occupy her time alone.

"I want Gabriel!" Chad wailed during the drive to Lac du Bonnet, to which his older brother snapped irritably, "Shut up, you stupid baby. He hates us!" Chad's response was to wail all the more.

Lisa Penner was standing on the school steps directing the students as they arrived. Spotting Chad clinging tearfully to Susannah, she bent down and smiled. "You are going to be in my class, Chad."

She wiped at his tears. "Did you know that I already know your mom? That sort of makes us not strangers, doesn't it?"

She stood up, holding his small hand in hers and winked pleasantly at Susannah. "Come on into the class and meet your new friends. Mom will be here at the end of the day when school is over."

Susannah smiled back gratefully. She could not

help liking Lisa. She could see how Gabriel would find comfort with Lisa.

If Lisa was aware that Susannah was no longer seeing him, she hid it well. She simply gave Susannah a comforting nod of encouragement as she led Chad into the school.

Calvin, on the other hand, stubbornly refused to permit his mother to escort him to his class. "Mom, you said I'm in Room 16. I can read numbers, okay?" Off he went without so much as a backwards glance.

Thinking to meander about Lac du Bonnet without the responsibility of her sons, and having nothing else to do, Susannah headed down the sidewalk to the main street. About to cross the road, she stopped dead.

Gabriel Desjarlais strode out of the Post Office. Noticing her, he too stopped. They stared across the expanse of the street at one another, neither moving or making a sound.

Her heart in her mouth, Susannah waited for him to walk away. He remained rooted to where he stood.

Fearing her knees might buckle beneath her, she wheeled around and hurried to her car. Safely inside, she leaned against the seat and took several deep breaths, trying to stop the shaking in her limbs. She was either going to have to get used to bumping into him or turn into a reclusive hermit. Starting up the engine with shaking hands, she drove back to the shelter of her cottage.

The Indian summer disappeared with September, and the leaves correspondingly turned and fell, carpeting Susannah's lawn with their bright oranges and yellows and leaving the trees barren.

She loved the sound of them crunching beneath her feet as she toiled in the yard, covering up the rose bushes with dried leaves and burlap to protect them from frost. The remaining less temperamental perennials received a raking over.

Bert was up and about more and walked over often to give Susannah advice. He told her how to cover her windows with heavy clear plastic to block the vestiges of wind, which would whistle their way through the window frames when the bitter winter weather arrived. He also recommended a local heating company to install baseboard heaters to keep the cottage warm.

With the foliage gone, the Semchuk cottage was now clearly visible from Susannah's front porch. Unfortunately, hers was equally visible, particularly from the river, causing her to feel exposed as she worked about the yard. She carefully kept her eyes averted from the river and Gabriel's home, which was also easier to see.

To Susannah's shock, Steven's parents appeared on her back porch one frosty morning. "We realized that if we had to wait for an invitation, our grandsons would be grown men before we saw them again," Mrs. James explained half-jokingly as she stepped past her daughter-in-law into the kitchen. She was a tall, thin woman who hid her sage and loving heart beneath a severe exterior.

Mr. James, a short, squat man, followed in behind his wife. His eyes revealed his pleasure at seeing Susannah much more than did his shy smile and ineffectual hand clasp.

Her apprehension at seeing her in-laws again evaporated as they calmly reentered her life without questions or expectations. Having taken the initial step, they were content to let Susannah dictate where things went from there.

Her father-in-law and Bert hit it off immediately and whiled away the weekend playing cards with

Calvin and Chad.

Initially, Ada and Mrs. James were cautious with one another, each intimidated by the other: one loud and boisterous, the other cool to the point of frostiness. It was their forthrightness which was their common ground and upon which they eventually built an understanding.

The boys did bring up Gabriel's name once or twice, but Susannah fielded any questions by portraying him as a concerned neighbour who had happily allowed Bert and Ada to take over as companions. Susannah could tell by her mother-in-law's lowered eyebrow that she did not fully buy Susannah's explanation, but she said nothing.

All too soon, the day came for her in-laws to return to Winnipeg. As he climbed into his car, Mr. James passed Susannah a notice which he claimed to have got from Bert. It was an advertisement for a trained Black Labrador dog. "I know Bert and Ada keep an eye on you, but I'd feel better if you had some protection."

Susannah promised to give the kennel a call as she kissed him goodbye. Mrs. James, on the other hand, was less subtle in giving Susannah advice. Standing beside the car, she gave her a hard stare. "Steven would expect you to resume your life, Susannah." Her voice was crisp and brittle. "I can see that you have made a nice little life for yourself and my grandsons, but it's obvious you aren't complete. I wish you to know that while we understand no one could ever replace Steven, life is no good if it's empty." She gripped Susannah by the shoulders. "I sincerely hope you won't hold yourself back from finding love again."

Whether Mrs. James was exceptionally perceptive or had been educated by Ada, Susannah could not tell, but the woman's strength pierced her heart. There was so much Susannah longed to say to this woman in whom she had always had so much difficulty confiding, but the words could only find expression in the gripping embrace she gave her.

She kept her word to Mr. James, calling the kennel the following morning. An appointment was arranged, and the next weekend, Susannah packed up the boys and drove to the address she had been given.

"That was Gabriel's house!" Calvin screeched as they rounded a bend.

"How do you know that?" she asked, nervous, curious.

"Cause he was outside, and we waved at him."

"Did he wave back?"

"He sure did!" both boys cried excitedly.

She was glad she had been too busy watching for a kennel sign to have noticed him. She found the kennel and parked the car. When she saw the family name posted on the sign outside the kennel's large aluminum sided building, she nearly turned around and drove away. Kaminski. That would explain the K in K-Kennels, she thought ruefully.

The situation became even more unnerving when Dawn Kaminski came out to welcome them, clad in skin-tight jeans.

"Hi! When Dad said who was coming to look at Bodger, I couldn't believe my ears." She smiled down at Calvin and Chad. "So Mom's going to buy you a dog, eh?"

She led them into the building and out back to a large, outdoor dog run. "Bodger!" she called out. Immediately, a robust Black Lab came bounding over to the gate.

He licked the boys excitedly when Dawn let him

out and wagged his tail as he sniffed at Susannah. "We trained him for some prospective owners who at the last minute decided they didn't want him and stiffed us with the bill. He's good-natured," she went on, "and you can have him at cost. We'll throw in the training as a freebie."

When Susannah informed her she would like to see the dog spend more time with the boys before making up her mind, Dawn invited her to a cup of coffee.

"So Gabriel Desjarlais dumped you along with the rest of us?" Dawn said as she stirred her coffee and leaned against the picnic table Susannah was seated at.

Susannah frowned.

"Hey! Don't worry about it. I know it hurts. He's such a wonderful hunk of meat. Trouble is, he never stays with any woman long. Lisa Penner was the longest. Two years that went on. Everybody figured it was wedding bells, and then poof! She's in tears, and he's bringing some model back from Toronto."

"Bodger, down!" Dawn commanded with a raised arm when he had excitedly jumped up and knocked Chad off his feet. The dog readily complied with the command, and Chad stood back up, giggling merrily. "Me, I've been after him since high school." She grinned. "So now you know what an old bag I am. Anyway, that's why I'm always a little testy the first time I meet his latest interest."

So, Gabriel wasn't seeing Lisa or Dawn, Susannah thought happily. Not that it made any difference, of course. It was just nice to know.

"I must say though," Dawn said with a pause, "I am surprised you didn't get him to the altar. He was nuts about you. Everyone knew about Gabriel's Susannah." She finished wistfully, "I don't know what it is. Maybe he's afraid of commitment or something."

Susannah grimaced at the knowledge that people believed he had dumped her. But, when all was said and done, did it matter what people thought? If anything, it preserved their perception of Gabriel being carefree.

She found herself warming to Dawn despite herself. Why was she surprised? Gabriel was a very special person; would he not date equally special women? Sometimes their exteriors might be a little rough around the edges, as in Dawn's case, but the Toronto model was probably every bit as soft-hearted as Dawn and Lisa.

Maybe he had been sincere when he had dated these women and was not the callous cavalier people envisioned. Maybe he was simply an honest man in search of the right woman. Hadn't he said he had never loved anyone except herself?

A vision of him bending to kiss her flashed across her eyes. Startled, she jumped to her feet. "He appears to be a fine dog," she said.

They made the required transactions, and Dawn offered free advice anytime Susannah needed. A short time later they piled into Susannah's car, the new addition to the family eagerly slurping his young masters' faces.

On the return trip, Gabriel's house was pointed out by Calvin and Chad as she drove past, but she carefully kept her eyes on the road, fearing the possibility of seeing him. The boys dejectedly informed her that he was nowhere to be seen.

With November came the snow, blanketing everything with a glistening glow of white. Susannah was working on a piece of crocheting Ada had been patiently teaching her. It was proving to be a challenge, but she needed something to fill the time. Looking up from her work, she noticed Ada trudging across the yard, her large legs leaving gaping holes in the freshly fallen snow. Setting aside her hook, she went to put on a pot of coffee.

"Well, I can't stand no more of this," Ada announced as she stomped the snow off her boot and onto the doormat.

Susannah laughed, thinking her neighbour was referring to winter.

"It's no laughing matter, girl," Ada said sternly as she took a seat at the kitchen table.

Susannah's eyes widened in genuine surprise.

"I mean you and Gabriel Desjarlais. I have no intention of watching the two of you ruin everyone's Christmas with your stubborn pride."

"Ada, Gabriel and I have long since ended things between us."

"You mean, you ended things," Ada accused severely.

"Well, I ... uh ... yes."

"It doesn't matter. I've harped at Gabriel all along that he should give in and come see you. I can't decide which of you is more stubborn."

"Ada, I did what I thought was best."

"Hmpf!" Ada snorted, resting her enormous breasts on folded arms. "You think I don't know what happened? It wasn't no coincidence that I bring old Bert home from the hospital after you and Gabriel save his life, and suddenly there's no more Gabriel." She swilled her coffee. "For a while, me and Bert felt kind of like it was our fault, except we can't help him being sick. That's just the way things are."

Susannah stared down at her feet, avoiding Ada's eyes. Ada pressed. "Every time Bert comes here to help you with something, it shortens the time he has left. He ain't supposed to be doing none of those things."

"No!" Susannah looked up, horrified at her selfishness, unwitting as it was.

"I could stop him from coming over. I'm certainly big enough." Ada stopped for a necessary breath. "You wanna know why I don't?"

Susannah slowly nodded her head.

"Because it's worse to watch him live half a life. I'd rather see him enjoy what's left of his time than drag it out a little bit longer by tying him to his armchair while he wastes away because he ain't living. If feeling useful to you and your boys is a bright spot in his life, then I leave him to it." She stood up. "That's lovin' your man, Susannah."

Bending over, she smothered Susannah in her ample, pillow-like arms. Susannah began to cry softly, and Ada patted her head. "There, there. Everything's gonna be alright. Life is meant to be lived, Susannah. None of us can lock up our hearts. If we do, we have nothing left."

Thirteen

Susannah removed the fur coat from its hanger. Putting it on, she could not resist running her hand along its soft, smooth pelt. It had been her last anniversary present from Steven. Stepping outside, she shivered from the cold and the knowledge that it was a steady, minus thirty-three degrees Celsius with a biting wind. Pulling up the collar to protect her face, she hurried up the road to where her car waited.

She started up the engine before unplugging the block heater from the electrical outlet. Allowing the car to warm up for a few minutes, she leaned her head against the back of the seat. Did she have the courage to follow through with her plan?

The warm air from her deep sigh filled the windshield with its white steam and turned immediately into frost. Turning on the defroster, she slumped her chin on the steering wheel. Maybe she should just go on back inside and forget this.

What if Ada was wrong? What if Gabriel no longer loved her? No, she told herself, love couldn't be turned on and off like a light switch. He would still be in love with her.

The question was, would he be willing to give it a second try? He did not have a reputation for seeing the same woman twice, although by the possessive way Dawn spoke of him on occasion, she suspected he and Dawn enjoyed a casual, on-again-off-again relationship.

The two women had hit it off. Susannah had initially called Dawn to ask a few questions regarding Bodger and wound up inviting Dawn over. The friendship had taken its own course from there. Susannah knew that in the past Gabriel had only seen Dawn for a few months, but she was also well aware that if he felt the need for a woman, it would likely be the willing arms of Dawn he would go to.

Deciding the engine had warmed sufficiently, Susannah started off down the road, the car sluggish in its response. The tires made an odd plopping sound created by the flat spot where they had rested on the road in the extreme cold for a few hours.

The road had been recently snow ploughed, making Susannah's drive reasonably easy. A few minutes later she slowed her car and pulled onto the drive to Gabriel's home. There was no way to tell if anyone was inside the house and no vehicles were visible.

Parking at the end of the drive between the house and a large aluminum Quonset, she turned off the engine and sat back, procrastinating over ringing the doorbell. Sighing deeply, she opened the door and put a booted foot onto the snow. It's not too late to turn back, she told herself as she brought out the other foot.

Climbing the wide steps that led to a massive wooden verandah which wrapped around the house, she sought once more for the words she might say. As had been the case for the past two days, nothing came to mind. She had settled on saying whatever came out of her mouth when the time actually came, but now she wished she were better prepared.

Pressing the doorbell, she stamped the snow from her boots.

"Why, Susannah, what a lovely surprise!" Mrs. Desjarlais exclaimed upon opening the door. "Please, come in."

"Mrs. Desjarlais, I ..." Susannah began.

"Please, Susannah, come in. I'm sure you're cold," Mrs. Desjarlais interrupted. "Give me your coat and take off your boots. I'll make some coffee."

"Mrs. Desjarlais ..." Susannah began again.

"I know, you've come to see Gabriel." She smiled. "He's gone out for awhile but should be back soon. Come sit and have coffee with me."

Susannah followed Mrs. Desjarlais through to the kitchen, passing a comfortable living room and then an elaborate dining room.

The kitchen was a typically enormous farm kitchen, its modern appliances gleaming spotlessly. Mrs. Desjarlais indicated a table at the end of the kitchen and Susannah sat down. The table was surrounded on both sides by large expanses of ceiling to floor windows which looked out over the farm. A solarium, extending from the family room at the rear of the kitchen and lush with vegetation, was visible from where she sat.

"Are you the one who makes the solarium so beautiful?"

Mrs. Desjarlais smiled. "Yes. Gabriel built that for me a few years ago. He tells me you enjoy gardening as well."

Susannah sipped her coffee. "I don't know very much about it. I only started this summer, but, yes, I do like it."

"And what do you do with yourself now that the snow has covered everything?"

"Ada's teaching me to crochet, but I must be

honest, I don't think I'm going to do as well with it as the gardening." Susannah laughed.

"Gabriel will be happy you've come," his mother said suddenly. "We haven't heard him whistling his little Susannah song for a long time."

Susannah looked up, startled at the woman's directness. She avoided a response by taking another sip of coffee.

"He's been very sad."

Susannah brought her eyes up to Mrs. Desjarlais's. If she could be so forward, then so could Susannah. "Mrs. Desjarlais, why did you never remarry?"

"Ah. Ada told me that was the problem." Going to the counter to refill their mugs, she looked back at Susannah. "Plenty of local men were interested. I'm not so ugly, that's for sure."

Laughing she placed the mugs on the table and returned to her seat. "After Gabriel's father, no one stirred my heart the way he had. Gabriel is much like him. But if someone had ..."

Taking Susannah's hand, she gently patted it. "I would not have hesitated. Even with all my children and grandchildren, I am lonely sometimes."

Letting go, she laughed. "Who knows? Maybe when I retire and travel a little bit, I'll meet some doddering old fool who wouldn't mind doddering with me."

Looking out the window, she pointed. "Here comes Gabriel now."

With a churning stomach, Susannah turned to see his truck stop beside her car. Getting out, he put his hands on his hips and stood looking at it. Raising his head, he saw Susannah and his mother looking at him from the kitchen, and then he turned and walked into the Quonset.

Susannah's heart sank. Avoiding his mother's

eyes, she put her mug to her mouth with both hands and took a long draught.

"He just wants you to come out there where you will have some privacy," his mother said softly.

"What if you're wrong?" Susannah asked uneasily.

"I know my son. Even if I were wrong, are you going to give up without a fight?"

Susannah stood outside the door to the Quonset, fighting the urge to turn and run. Twisting the doorknob, she pushed it open and stepped inside.

Gabriel was bent over, under the hood of his Corvette, vigorously twisting something. He had not heard her enter.

"Gabriel," she called out, her voice raspy.

Slowly putting down a wrench, he turned.

Susannah quivered beneath his cold stare. Why hadn't she run away when she had the chance? She couldn't think what to say. Her voice squeaked. "I made a mistake." Tears were threatening to choke out her voice. "Maybe the biggest mistake of my life."

He expelled a long sigh before picking up the rag which rested on the car. Wiping the grease from his hands, he leaned against the car and waited for her to continue, his face unreadable and as hard as stone.

Susannah lifted a shaking hand to her brow and unconsciously massaged it. This was unbearably difficult. "I guess I'm just used to taking everyone in my life for granted. I never considered how I might hurt you, or Calvin and Chad. I only saw my own pain. I didn't want to ever hurt again the way I had when Steven died."

He put down the rag, and turning his back to her, walked to a sink beside a work bench and ran his hands under the water with a bar of soap. Turning off the water, he picked up a clean rag and strode to the work bench. Facing her, he leaned against it, crossed his legs, wiped his hands and raising an eyebrow at her, waited for more.

"The problem was, I ended up hurting anyway. It's been hell without you."

He set the cloth on the bench and continued staring at her in silence.

"I'm sorry I hurt you just to save myself some pain I might never have had in the first place." She placed a hand over her mouth in an attempt to hold back the sobs which nearly escaped. "You once called me a little girl. People always call me that, and now I know why. I've never had to be grown-up before." She paused to control her breathing. "If you could bring yourself to forgive me, maybe we could start over." Her voice dropped to a whisper. "If it's not too late."

Gabriel unbuttoned the greasy lumberjack shirt he was wearing and pulled it off, revealing a clean sweatshirt underneath.

His continued silence spoke volumes. It was over. It had ended the day she had asked him to leave. Tears streaming down her face, Susannah turned to the door. "I guess it's too late."

Her hand was on the door when his voice came across the Quonset. "I kind of like you being a little girl once in awhile."

She whirled around.

His face was still unreadable, and he was drumming his fingers against the bench. "The thing is, Susannah," he said slowly, his voice measured, "I've had a lot of time to think, and I've got a few conditions that I didn't have before. Maybe my mistake was in letting you call all the shots."

Susannah dared to grasp at the tiny ray of hope.

She wiped beneath her eyes and waited. Anything. His conditions could be anything, and she would meet them. He would never ask for anything unreasonable.

"I'm through with having girlfriends." He paused for emphasis. "I want a wife."

Did he mean anybody, or would she do?

"Also, the farm would have to become your career. I need help here on the farm. Maybe just in the form of companionship. It's long, irregular hours. I need to know there's someone there when I'm done and need to talk things over. However, there's lots of work in the greenhouses and such ... if you want ... but I wouldn't expect it of you."

Susannah cupped her hands over her mouth. He did mean her. He was asking her to marry him! She had come hoping to convince him to see her again, and he had surpassed that hope.

"And there's one last thing." He looked hard at her. "I love Calvin and Chad like my own sons, but I want more than two kids. I want babies. Lots of them."

Lots of them? Susannah's voice was shaking. "Could we start with one or two and take it from there?"

Gabriel grinned. "Does that mean we have an agreement?"

Yes, she could meet his conditions, eagerly! She nodded her head.

He cocked his head to one side and folded his arms over his chest. "Then why are you still standing way over there?"

A screech of delight burst from Susannah as she ran towards him and threw herself into his waiting arms. Gabriel lifted her up and twirled her around as they both laughed.

As he let her down, still holding her against him, she cupped his face in her hands, relishing the roughness of it. "Gabriel Desjarlais, that was the most unromantic marriage proposal I have ever heard of!" She giggled.

His eyes danced. "We'll have plenty of time for romance."

"Ha! You were simply tormenting me."

He laughed. "I confess. And I loved it!"

"And I love you," she confessed.

He held her at arms length. "And I love you," he said hoarsely, his eyes dark as he bent to kiss her.

A few moments later, while kissing the hair he had unpinned, he murmured, "There's one more condition I forgot to mention."

"What's that?"

Gabriel lifted her chin. "You do recall Ada saying I'm not known for my restraint when it comes to women?"

"Yes."

"Well, after the past three and a half tortuous months of waiting for you, I think a long engagement will be the death of me."

Susannah giggled. "Just how short an engagement did you have in mind?"

"Let's put it this way. I'd like to celebrate Christmas as a family."

"Christmas is barely three weeks away!"

"Then we'd better get right to work."

"Did you say you were waiting for me?"

Gabriel gave her a slow smile. "I was."

"How could you know I would change my mind? It was firmly made up."

He laughed. "Like I told you at the start, I know when a woman's crazy about me."

"Give me a serious answer," she pressed.

His eyes grew sombre. "I knew how much we loved each other. I also knew that if we had any chance at all of making it last, you were going to have to be completely over Steven. Being willing to love again was part of it."

"What if I had been too stubborn?"

"That was a chance I had to take. The way it was, you would have always held back a piece of yourself. I would never have had all of you. I realized that the day you sent me away. That's also why I never tried to see you again."

Susannah grinned. "That broke my heart, you know. I thought that you could have at least tried to get me back. Remember that day in Lac du Bonnet when you came out of the Post Office?"

Gabriel nodded.

"If you had spoken to me then, I would have melted completely."

He shrugged his shoulders. "You weren't ready. I could see it in your eyes."

"I'm ready now." She tiptoed her fingers up the front of his shirt and peeped coyly at him. "You didn't run to any other woman for comfort?"

"You tell me," he said as he embraced her, his kiss passionate and demanding. When he pulled his mouth from hers, he whispered, "There's never been any other woman for me but you, Susannah."

"I believe you," she answered dizzily and short of breath, her head swimming.

Taking her hand, he laughed. "Let's go find my mother. She'll be relieved. I think my moodiness was beginning to get on her nerves."

Susannah stepped out the door he held open. "I think Steven's mother will be relieved as well. She suspected there was a man but knew I would be too stubborn to answer any questions."

They ran together across the yard, arm in arm, Gabriel whistling "Oh Susannah."

She pulled him back before they went inside and narrowed her eyes at him. "Say! This hasn't all been some elaborate scheme to get my cottage for your mother, has it?"

"Definitely." Gabriel chuckled, giving her a long kiss, neither one feeling the cold wind swirling about them.

Epilogue

Susannah checked her sons' faces for traces of breakfast before opening the front door.

"Hurry up and don't make the bus wait," she said as she kissed first Chad and then Calvin goodbye. Bodger at their side, they ran down the drive towards the road, arriving mere seconds before the bus came into view. They turned back to wave at Susannah and at Gabriel who had come to stand behind her.

"Brr!" Susannah muttered as she closed the door against the bitterly cold February morning.

Gabriel placed an affectionate hand on her shoulder as he bent to give her a kiss.

Susannah accepted his kiss before raising an eyebrow at him. "And just where do you think you're going?" she asked as she barred the door with her arms.

Looking surprised, he grinned at her. "Out to the greenhouses. Have I forgotten something?"

She gave him a secret smile. "No, but we do need to have a little chat."

His confusion and concern apparent, he asked, "Is something wrong, Susannah?"

"No, something's terribly right."

She unfastened the buttons of his parka. "Do you remember my saying that I was hoping your belated

New Year's present would arrive soon?"

He nodded.

"Do you remember the third condition you insisted upon before agreeing to marry me?"

Gabriel nodded slowly and then broke into a broad smile. "Really?"

Her beaming face answered for her.

He threw back his dark head in a booming laugh which filled the house. "Really?" he asked again.

Susannah nodded her auburn head. He laughed again.

"When?"

"Mid September."

Gabriel removed his parka. "I guess I had better get to work on converting a room into a nursery. But first ..." He grabbed her by the arm and pulled her towards the stairs. "I've got a great idea for how we can celebrate."

He tugged her up along behind him and headed down the hall towards their bedroom.

Susannah giggled. "You always want to celebrate everything the same way."

Gabriel opened the door and sweeping her into his arms, carried her through it. "Is that a complaint?"

"Never!" Susannah replied, giving him a kiss to prove she meant what she said.

ABOUT THE AUTHOR

SELENA MINDUS has lived on the Canadian prairies most of her life. She's well-traveled but still thinks that there's no place like the big skies of the wheatfields. She loves the great outdoors, which comes in handy since her life with an adventurous husband and two rough-and-tumble boys has led Selena to live a bit on the wild side herself. She's done everything from motocross and snowmobiling to hunting and parasailing. The men in her life are now talking about sky-diving, but Selena insists there are some limits to what she'll do.

Don't miss out on the latest news from Ponder Romance!

"Ponderings"

Ponder Romance's biannual newsletter, featuring the newest Ponder Romance, the latest of delightful escapades by the very romantic, Dominick Miserandino, and much more! Complete the reader survey below and we'll put you on our newsletter mailing list!

Please circle the appropriate answer/fill in blanks:

1. Was this the first Ponder Romance you've read? *yes/no*
2. Which novel did you read?...............................
3. On a scale of 1-5, *(1 poor, 5 excellent)* how would you rate the novel you read? ....
4. Was there anything in particular you did not enjoy?

....
5. Was there anything you especially liked?.............

....
6. What is your opinion of the cover?......................
7. How often do you read romance novels? *regularly, occasionally, rarely*
8. Would you read another Ponder Romance? *yes/no*
9. Where did you obtain this Ponder Romance?.....
10. Your age: *under 18, 18-25, 26-34, 35-50, over 50*

Name

Address

City   State/Prov.   Country

Code

Mail to:

Ponder Publishing Inc.	Ponder Publishing Inc.
PO Box 23037, RPO McGillivray	60 East 42nd Street, Suite 1166
Winnipeg, MB R3T 5S3	New York, NY 101655
Canada	USA